The Marriage Feast

The Marriage Feast

Pär Lagerkvist

ʬ HILL AND WANG NEW YORK
A division of Farrar, Straus and Giroux

NOTE

*

All the stories in this volume have been translated by Alan Blair, with the following exception: "On the Scales of Osiris," which was translated by Carl Eric Lindin

CONTENTS

*

The Marriage Feast

JONAS and Frida were to be married at four o'clock in the afternoon, and the guests were beginning to collect at the little house on the outskirts of the village by the railway where the ceremony was to take place. Ponies and traps came from the surrounding countryside, where one or two distant relatives of Frida lived—Jonas hadn't any—and there were also several people from the village itself. It seemed they would be about fifteen, all told.

It was a lovely day and the men were outside, strolling in the little garden, shaking hands with each other, standing talking, or taking a turn around the house as though they were looking it over. On the east gable was a faded sign over a small doorway:

Frida Johansson
Haberdasher

Hm. Well, well, so Frida was getting off today. Aha. That was all they said, but their tone implied a lot.

Hm, it was a funny thing about this wedding, but there would be the usual food and drink anyway, and they might just as well be there, seeing they were invited. So they thought about going in.

The bridegroom was standing on the steps. He was a thick-set, insignificant little man, with a fair, drooping moustache and a continual happy smile—he was always smiling. He had clear, kind, almost grateful eyes, and he blinked a lot, almost as though to keep out of the way. He was apt to hold his head rather on one side, as if he were listening. He had a very pleasing appearance, he had indeed. His real name was Jonas Samuelsson; but he was usually called Jonas Gate, owing to his habit of always hanging about down by the level-crossing gate in his younger days, in case anyone off the train wanted a hand with the luggage. It had thus been quite some time before he had turned his hand to any steady job, but he had been porter at the hotel for a long time now, so his standing down by the level-crossing gate was all in order. It was his profession. As to that, of course, he was going to marry Frida today, so it was harder now to say what he was, or thought of being: whether he would help her in the shop if need be, or even give up work altogether. There was no telling what Frida's plans were, or how much she had been able to scrape together. No one had any idea. Maybe it was quite a tidy sum. But she might just as well let him stay on down there, it suited him somehow. He wasn't a particularly go-ahead chap.

The relatives didn't really like the idea of Frida's going and getting married in this way, and it wasn't surprising. Not that they cared what she let herself in for—that was her lookout. But there was no need to go and get married at her age; it was unnecessary, they thought. And she had always been one to save a bit—not that *they* knew anything about that, it was nothing to do with them. But now that she *was* going to at last, she might have chosen someone other than Jonas. Not that there were so many to choose from, of course. However, Frida was one of them, after all, and came of quite good family, so it did seem strange that she could put up with him. Well, well, that was her business; she wanted it that way, well and good. He was certainly a nice, good-natured sort of chap, that he was. No one could say he wasn't.

Jonas was standing on the porch receiving the guests and looking around obligingly as though wondering if there were something he could carry. And if someone arrived with a coat that he had had on in the gig, or with anything at all, he was delighted to help carry it in. It was something he could do, and on a day like this a man is only too glad to show what he is capable of. It was worse once all the guests had arrived, for no one spoke to him and he just stood there, still smiling, with his arms hanging beside his new black suit, which Frida had had made for the occasion. He had nothing in particular to do, but as usual he looked contented all the same.

It was better after a while when it was time for coffee and he could find chairs for everyone and beamingly invite them to sit up to the table. He said nothing; he preferred only to speak when he had to. He did think of asking them to be sure and have more buns and cakes, but he thought better of it; they were Frida's, after all. The guests helped themselves, all the same, and over their second cups began talking and feeling more at home. Jonas was delighted; he stood beside the mantelpiece with his cup of coffee, listening to all that was said with the most heartfelt good-will; ran out into the kitchen to fill up the coffee-pot, handed round the sugar to the women at the tables by the window, and generally made himself useful. Of course, it wasn't usual for the bridegroom to do the waiting like that, but he probably didn't know. They smiled at him in their own way, and he gave them his sweet smile in return. They may have thought he was rather silly with that smile of his, but one couldn't say that, because it was both wise and kind. It was just that he never stopped smiling. Well, that was his way. He was thinking now how well it was all going—it was too, there wasn't a hitch.

Up in the attic Frida was sitting being dressed as a bride. Agnes Karlsson, her best friend as they say, was pinching Frida's thin hair around the tongs so that there was a smell of burning right out through the window. It was the first time Frida had had her hair curled, but then it was the thing to do. She hardly recognized herself as she looked in the bureau mirror that she had had moved up.

She was not very like the old Frida, which was as it should be on such a festive day.

Oh, just think of its being today! Today that she and Jonas were to stand in front of the altar and be joined in matrimony forever and ever before their God. To think that that day was really here, and that it was to happen soon, in a little while.

"I hope they have arranged the flowers properly down there, as I said, beside the stools. Do you think they have, Agnes?"

"Oh yes, they'll have done that all right."

"And do you think the wedding cake has arrived safely, the one with our initials?"

"Yes, it's sure to have come. I saw Klas arriving with a cake box—that was probably it."

"Supposing you were to go down just to make sure?"

"Good heavens, we must get this finished."

"Yes, of course, that's very important. Everything is important on a day like this; one must think of everything."

Oh, if only everything goes off all right, and it's the kind of festival she has hoped for, that she has dreamed about so much. If only it's all as the great solemnity of the occasion demands.

What is there on earth greater than two people being made one, meeting before God to have their compact sealed at the throne of the Eternal One? Alas, there were no doubt many who never gave a thought to what kind of festival this really was, looked on it as a gay party where they could dance and laugh. Which it was as well; of course, she herself was so happy that she was dancing inside. No bride could be happier than she, and none had more reason to be. No, none.

And yet, in spite of everything, in spite of all this joy— it was nevertheless the solemnity she felt most of all. The great solemnity that lay over this day of theirs. What they were now faced with was the most momentous thing that could happen to her and Jonas. Their lives were to be united, they were to be made one, their souls were to be joined together for ever. Neither of them would be lonely any more, neither she nor Jonas. How strange it was, never to be lonely any more. She knew what it meant, she who had been alone ever since her parents died when she was a child. She had been made to know so well what it was, every day of her life. No, it is not good for man to live alone.

Was it strange then, that at this glorious moment she wanted everything to be as worthy and beautiful as possible?

"Take a look in the mirror and see what you think," Agnes said.

And Frida leaned forward and looked at her reflection, stroked her forehead, touched her unfamiliar hair.

How small and thin her face was; she looked like a girl with anaemia. But her features were worn and her cheeks were sunken. The years had put their mark on her, she had so many wrinkles; but it was all so delicate and fine, it all seemed to have been carefully done. Even a scar on her neck seemed small and delicate, like everything else about her. Only her eyes were large, infinitely gentle and artless, and strangely wide open. Her mouth looked like a thin line, as though she had been a very determined and enter-prising woman, but that was only because it was so thin and just as pale as the rest. It was when she smiled that it became transformed. It was extraordinary; her whole face lit up at once. Also she had the nicest false teeth in the whole district; there were many who thought so if it came to that. They fitted so well.

No, she was not beautiful. She never had been and now it was no longer to be expected. But there was something unusually pure about her, as is often the way with seam-stresses and laundresses. She had done sewing for many years before setting up her shop, and there, too, she always had to do with clean and delicate things. She was so well suited to them, which is probably why she had taken to it. Her hands were quite white, since she had never had to do any rough work, but she had worked hard with them just the same; one could see that.

"What about trying on the coronet," Agnes said, "so that we can see if the hair suits it? You say you want to have it."

"Yes, Agnes dear, do."

So Agnes fastened it on to the top of Frida's head with hairpins, a little coronet of myrtle which Frida had woven so neatly out of a myrtle she had inherited from her mother, who had used it when she was a bride. Three times it had died out, but she had taken cuttings, so it was the same tree really. The inside of the coronet was filled with white tulle, which billowed out in a lovely veil.

Frida stood up to see herself properly in the mirror. She had not yet put on her petticoat and dress, in order not to crease them, but her drawers were snow white and trimmed with the finest lace in the whole shop; the veil fell light and airy down her back, right to her knees. She was really very sweet standing there admiring herself, so thoughtful and happy. She looked at her reflection with dreamy eyes, seeing herself for the first time as a bride.

"You've nothing on but your drawers!" Agnes exclaimed, and burst out laughing.

She hadn't, either. Frida smiled gently as she realized it, then held the veil aside and carefully sat down again.

Agnes thought the coronet was too flat on the head.

"No, do you think so? I hadn't thought of it. Yes, perhaps it's not quite right."

"Supposing we curled the hair a bit more, so that it sits a little higher? But it's not so easy to get it up any higher, you see."

"No, it's so thin, isn't it?"

"Yes, that's just the trouble, but I'll have a try."

So Agnes very kindly started all over again; she took hair from the sides and got it up on top, although it wouldn't really reach, and then had the idea of putting the knot up there, too, for it didn't matter where it was, seeing that the veil would hide it anyway. She was so kind and helpful.

And during all this Frida sat there in a dream, which was not strange. . . .

She was thinking of how she and Jonas had met, how their destinies had been linked together, their steps guided forward to this great and glorious hour. They had been fond of each other for a long, long time, goodness knows how many years. It was a secret harmony of their souls, without words, without their being aware of it themselves. It had not blossomed into real love until later on, but they had, as it were, come closer to one another, even so. She remembered how he had taken her suitcase once when she had come off the train from town. They had walked along the street and he had said, "I suppose you have been in to do some shopping," and she had said, "Yes, I have," but as she said it she had happened to look into his eyes. That was four years ago now, but she remembered as though it were yesterday. That was when it had started in earnest.

Yes, how strange everything is, people's destinies—what is it that guides us? What had brought her and Jonas together to this sacred feeling that they would never be parted again?

But still a long time passed before there was anything said between them. That's the way of it. Oh, this deceptive game of love, this sweet game of hide-and-seek played by two people in love. The feelings of both are the same, but neither will admit it. Their souls are drawn to each other, reach out to each other in ardent longing, call to each other like twittering birds, like animals in their stalls in the evening.

And mixed up with it all a constantly disquieting uneasiness, in spite of everything. I suppose he does love me. Perhaps he doesn't. And do I really love him, with all my heart, deep down inside, as one should? As one must? Is it ordained by God that we are two souls meant to meet during our wandering here, to enter into the shining abode of love? Are we chosen and fitted for it? Yes, yes, I will believe, I will believe!

Yes, she believed. She knew. She sat gazing in front of her in tranquil rapture, transported by happiness.

No, no two people on earth could have met in a nicer, more beautiful way than they had, she and Jonas. Her eyes grew moist as she thought of it, and her gaze grew remote as though she were looking at a far-off land.

Was she right? Yes, that's how it was; what they felt for each other was love. She had accepted him because she was fond of him. She loved for the sake of loving. And Jonas? He had said yes because he thought it was so boundlessly good of her to accept him. He had never imagined it; but as soon as he was allowed to, he loved her more than words can say. He had never loved anyone before because no one had asked him, and it wasn't really the sort of thing he could bring himself to ask. But to repeat, once given permission, he was the most ardent lover imaginable. He looked up to her as to something divine, something inconceivably good and beautiful. He could not imagine a more perfect being. She was as providence itself to him.

He had not bothered much about the fact that she had a little money, because he didn't understand much about that kind of thing. He used it so seldom. But of course it was very nice, seeing that everyone talked about it. He himself felt a kind of reverence at the thought of these things. It made everything even more wonderful, if possible.

As long as it didn't mean that he would no longer be

able to stand down by the level-crossing gate, because he would certainly miss that. He was used to it, and once one has got used to something, it's hard to go without. That was his profession, as it were. But if Frida thought it was beneath him to go on working he would just have to put up with it. It would probably be all right, even so. That was something he had not liked to ask her about in so many words. Time enough for that. He loved her, that was the main thing; he loved her more than he could say, and there was nothing he wouldn't do for her. He loved Frida for her own sake, and because it was *she* who had been good enough to bother about him.

That's how it was. It amounted to love on both sides.

Jonas, yes. . . . She thought of him, and the kind of man he was. Thought of when he had thrown his arms around her out in the woods last spring, and said that she was his most beautiful flower. He could indeed say so much that was remarkable, things that no one else could have thought of. He had great gifts, that was certain, which no one but she knew anything about.

Agnes stopped combing.

"There now, Frida, we won't do better than that," she said.

"Oh, my dear, it's lovely! Thank you so much."

They looked at the hair from all angles, and found that it now sat much better and as prettily as they could wish.

"Now I think we ought to hurry up and get your dress on."

"Yes, I suppose it's nearly time. . . . Oh, Agnes dear, you've no idea how strange it feels."

"Yes, it must."

"Just imagine being dressed as a bride—it's all like a dream. I can't really believe it's true."

"If I might suggest it," Agnes said, "you ought to wear your nice black dress instead, it suits you so well."

"Agnes dear, how can you! You're not serious!" Frida

looked at her in amazement, quite distressed that she could say anything so thoughtless. "A bride must have white, you know that; it's an occasion for joy."

"Yes, yes, I only meant—that's *my* opinion—but of course you must do just as you like."

So Frida had her way. It would have been strange if she hadn't, after getting herself the dress for this very moment, sitting up sewing it night after night. And all the dreams she had put into it. Agnes helped her put it on. It was all so beautifully ironed and mustn't be creased at all, and all the lace had to hang properly. But the petticoat was showing at the back. What were they to do—they would have to pin it up.

Agnes stopped to listen.

"The pastor must have come."

"Oh, it's not possible," Frida said softly, feeling herself grow pale.

"You can hear he has, no one's saying a word."

"Then we must get ready," Frida said very quietly.

Jonas knocked gently on the half-open door.

"The pastor has come," he whispered reverently.

"Jonas dear, is that you? You can't see me, not yet. In just half a minute, we're just fastening this up. The pastor is here, you said. The time has come then—fancy its hanging down like that—it's funny, isn't it? Dear Agnes, do try and hurry."

"Well, stand still then, so that I can get at it!"

"Yes, yes, of course I will. . . . What did the pastor say, Jonas?"

"The pastor—what did he say? Oh, he didn't say anything."

"Didn't you say how do you do to him?"

"No, I left the room when he arrived."

"Did you?"

"Yes, I thought I would come up here."

"Yes, it was good of you to come and tell me. Now I'll

just put the coronet on, then I'm ready. Jonas dear, are you sure everything is as it should be down there?"

"Yes, Frida dearest, I think everything's all right; it all looks so nice."

"Are the flowerpots in the right place?"

"Yes."

"And the lace cloths on the stools—Hulda won't have forgotten them?"

"No, they're there."

"And the cake? The cake, Jonas! Do you know definitely if it has come?"

"Well, I can't say for sure, but I did see Klas arrive with a cake box; I should think that was probably it."

"Yes, that must have been it. Oh, I hope everything will be all right, and just as it should be, on this great and wonderful day in our life. They did get something to eat with their coffee, Jonas?"

"Yes, indeed."

"You did ask them to help themselves?"

"There was no need, Frida dear."

"Now I think you're ready," Agnes said, giving her a final critical look of inspection.

"Am I! Oh, thank you, Agnes dear. You can come in now, Jonas dear, there's no need for you to go on standing there behind the door."

So Jonas came in. He stood dumbfounded with admiration at this radiant vision in the middle of the room, dazzlingly white and lovely; at his own darling Frida, the sight of whom filled him with an almost dizzy joy. He looked and looked at her with shining eyes, unable to believe it was true.

"Am I all right, dear?"

"Yes," he said, his voice thick and his eyes filling with tears, poor fellow. He couldn't say any more, just pressed and pressed her hand as though to thank her—over and over again.

"Then everything's all right," Frida whispered with a sob. "We can go down together." And she dried her eyes, holding her handkerchief in front of them so as not to show her emotion and how touched she was.

"The bridal bouquet!" cried Agnes, getting it out of the vase and drying it on a towel. It was of pink carnations and greenery.

"Oh, dear Agnes, thank you so much. Fancy forgetting! One forgets everything at a time like this."

And so down they went. Side by side, tightly pressed against each other. The coronet slipped a little to one side going down the stairs, but otherwise all was well. Their eyes were shining as they entered the bridal room, the little room with the sun shining in through the curtains. As they advanced between the guests, the women stared hard at them and the men cleared their throats. Up by the stools the pastor was waiting for them, severe and dignified. They stood in front of him like simple-hearted children, full of devout expectancy. He eyed them over his pince-nez, then opened the book and began to read.

"In the name of God the Father, God the Son, and God the Holy Ghost . . ."

They hung on his words. There could not have been two more attentive listeners, so afraid were they of missing a single word, so moved by the solemnity of the moment. Jonas did indeed smile as usual, but it was merely out of inexpressible reverence. He kept his head a little on one side in order to hear everything, and his hands were clasped together in implicit reliance on what was being said to him. Frida, too, held her hands tightly together with the bouquet between them, and looked at the pastor with trusting, humble gratitude.

Presently, when they had to kneel down, they thought that was the loveliest of all. The sun shone on them, on Frida's lovely white dress with the veil all around it that seemed to be made of light, and on Jonas in his brand-new clothes. They were kneeling right in front of the window, and so their eyes shone with an almost supernatural radiance. Around them were all the flowerpots. It was a moment full of light and beauty.

The others, of course, could not feel it in the same way. They were only there because they were invited. But God's word was being read out, so of course it was a solemn occasion. The women were a little weepy, as they always are at weddings, and everyone listened to the trembling voices answering the time-honoured questions. It was certainly nice being there when they knew them both so intimately—because up to a point they knew Jonas very well, too.

The pastor gave no address for them, nor was there any need for one. But he read Our Father and the Benediction, and they thought it had never sounded so beautiful; they were like two completely new prayers with memorable new words that applied only to them. Then he closed the book, and the moving ceremony was at an end. Frida and Jonas were wedded to each other for always.

Wine was handed around, and everyone drank with them; first the pastor, who wished them happiness, then all the others according to age and position or relationship. The sun shone on the glasses, they clinked and sparkled all at once, the entire little room had something so festive about it. In the middle of the guests, entirely surrounded, stood the bride, radiant with happiness. And beside her stood Jonas, smiling with every wrinkle of his kind face. They drank to him, too, and he held his glass extended between his fingertips as though he were holding out an extraordinary kind of flower. Everywhere were kindly eyes that must be thanked, and he kept bowing incessantly. A wave of warmth and cordiality flowed toward him such as he could never have imagined. Then it grew a little quieter, they all sat down at the window tables or over on the sofa and began talking among themselves, and he was left to himself in the middle of the floor, quite a lot to himself.

But the women took hold of Frida by the arm to say a few words more heartfelt than the mere congratulations.

"Well, Frida dear, now you have got what you wanted, so I suppose you are happy, aren't you?"

"Oh yes, thank you, Mrs Lundgren, I am indeed. I am as happy as it is possible for anyone to be."

"Yes, I suppose you are, Frida dear."

And all the relatives had to go up and talk to her for a moment.

"So you're married, Frida dear."

"Yes, Emma dear."

"Oh well, you never know how things will turn out."

"Yes, who would have thought it would be like this? But then we don't really know what's ahead of us."

"Oh," put in Miss Svensson from the tobacconist's, "I always thought that Frida would get married. I said many times that it's a wonder Frida Johansson doesn't get married. She could easily."

"Yes, that's just what I thought. My old man always used to say as we sat talking about the family, 'No, Frida will never get married.' But I thought, no, it's always best to wait and see, one never really knows for sure. Well, good luck, Frida dear, we are all so *glad* that you've managed it."

"Thank you, thank you, dear Matilda."

So the talk went on, Frida smiling and happy. After all, she had Jonas. They nodded at each other secretively, their gaze still obscured, the sacred words resounding within them. They were now a little apart from each other, but that didn't matter, it was only for a little while. And it was all going so well—she could see he thought so, too. Oh yes, everyone was so nice and kind. Some of them had come a long way in order to be present on this, their great day. Strange that there were so many gathered here just for their sake. There were so many conversations going on that it was hard to follow them, and one didn't know whom to listen to. And just think how festive it was when they had all come up and drunk their health.

Now there was the smell of cooking from the kitchen, and the women began wondering what it was they were going to have; it was sure to be roast meat, as was customary. Frida was sure to have only the best, and she could no doubt afford it. What her income was from the little shop no one could say. And Hulda was going to do the waiting, ah yes. And she had a lace apron, well I never.

The pastor came up and said he must be going. There was nothing much to wait for at a wedding like this, and he had so much work to do at home, routine office work as it is called. No, of course he didn't know who Frida was, and what she had to offer. How should he know?

Frida had hoped that he would stay. He is sure to, she had thought. It would make it all so festive. But he was obliged to go. Yes, of course, when he had such an awful lot to do; one can imagine a clergyman who is responsible for all that is most important in life, for the souls of so many people. Yes, there must be a lot of work, a lot that is not apparent. She thanked him for making this moment so sacred, for all the beautiful words he had read. Both she and Jonas went to the door with him, and Jonas helped him on with his coat and opened the gate leading out into the road, where he stood bowing until the pastor had disappeared through the trees.

Dinner was ready now, and they all sat down, the bridal pair in the principal seats in the centre of one side, and the others gathered around them for this banquet in honour of the newly married. The men were talking of a sewer which emptied out into the lake too near the village; they had been discussing it and were going to finish the subject, for the farmers didn't know what a fuss there had been about it at the meeting. But now they got their smörgåsbord and an aquavit and began to think about eating. There was plenty to choose from, dishes of every kind, and there was nothing wrong with the aquavit either, so they had another. They began to feel nice and cheery, as was fitting at a wedding. Now that old Frida was getting married, they must see that it was done properly, and eat and drink as much as they could when it was offered for once in a while.

"Come on, Jonas, have a stiffener, it won't hurt you."

"What, isn't he drinking?" shouted Emil of Östragård, Frida's second cousin, across the table. "I should think he needs one! Go on, have one, it'll put a tongue in your head."

And Jonas smiled and took it, though he didn't usually touch that kind of thing, but of course he must when they wanted him to join them.

"Well, to think it's come to a wedding. Who would have thought it!"

"Oh, more surprising things than this can happen. Sometimes they're in such a hurry that it makes you wonder what's wrong. No question of that in this case!"

"No, Julius, that it isn't! Cheers! You were always a wag!"

"No, by Christ, if they want to swap bullocks with me, then they'll have to bring along the best they have and still pay the difference. I told him so, too. No, it was the rottenest cattle-market I've ever been to."

"Didn't you even get a drink?"

"No, the place was shut."

"Oh well, then, of course you couldn't do any business."

"Hey there, Emil, fill them up here! You can't keep it all down your end!"

They went on drinking after the roast meat was brought in, and Jonas had to join in, though he didn't want to. "You're a damn queer sort of chap, not drinking." He was to have a drop in him, same as they. So Jonas drank, though he tried to have as little as possible. He was one of those people who just couldn't say no. And they all meant so well, wanting him to join in.

"Take a stiff one and get your strength up; you've got a good day's work ahead of you such as you never did in your life before, I'll bet!"

"You must at least have a good strong breath if Frida's to be satisfied with you."

"Well, you're in for a good time now, Jonas. No need for you to go and overwork in any way."

"Are you going to give up your job at the hotel? Oh, you don't know. Hasn't she said anything yet?"

"Perhaps you'll be selling embroidery in your old age. Well, not so bad either, a nice dainty job. And I suppose you'll have to go poking about here with all these flowers. Frida's got a frightful lot of flowerpots, that she has."

"What's the idea; is Jonas going to help in your shop, or what are you going to make him do?"

There was no need for Frida to answer; they were all talking at once and there was a terrific hubbub. She sat looking straight in front of her with her big, gentle eyes, the bridal coronet slightly askew, but dignified and calm in her white dress, which really suited her very well when you came to think of it. Now and then she would squeeze Jonas's hand under the table, and she would light up with a blissful smile as they looked at each other with secret joy. Then she would grow serious again, almost melancholy.

It was twilight now, and Hulda had to light the lamps. The sweet was brought in. It had turned out very well, but Frida could not eat much; she just tasted it to see that it was all right. Yes, of course, it was all right; they'd taken such trouble with it. And then came the cake. It was certainly very handsome. In the middle was a J and an F in bright red jam, but no one noticed it, and besides the letters were all intertwined. But she and Jonas saw it, and they gave each other a happy, tender look, and held each other's hand under the table. Wine was served with the cake. If the pastor had been able to stay he would probably have made a speech for them now, he would indeed. He could make a very good speech when he had to. But it all went very well notwithstanding and the cake was eaten up.

Afterwards there was to be coffee. They all got up from the table and spread out over the room, the men talking and booming, a little unsteady on their feet. Cigars were handed around and the coffee was poured out.

"Haven't you any brandy, Frida?" asked Emil.

No, that's something she had forgotten. It hadn't really occurred to her that they would drink so much on an occasion like this.

"Well, that's stingy when we're celebrating like this," Emil said. "It *is* a wedding, you know, so there ought to be some brandy, see! I've got a bottle out in the trap that I went and bought, so we can have that." And he lumbered out through the door, returning in a minute with the bottle.

"Now for a drop in the coffee!"

They started drinking. They shouted everything they said, as though they were standing out in the fields yelling across at each other from one farm to the next, and they all swore as though they were going to kill each other when they met, though they were firm friends standing close together, all talking at once. They became more and more drunk as the evening wore on, swaying against each other and sitting down heavily so that the chairs creaked. The ones from the village were a little more dignified—they had grown rather more superior—but those farmers were really too awful. The room was filled with fumes from the liquor and the warm smell of billowing smoke.

The women were having a nice time on their own. They had gathered in one corner and were talking about people

who were not there, and what had happened in the district
—there was quite a lot since last time, for there were not
so many parties nowadays. Then they spoke their minds,
shaking their heads, pursing their lips, whispering and
listening and repeating things, whatever it happened to be.
Frida sat with them for a while, then cast an eye into the
kitchen, rearranged the flowers that had not been put back
as they should, and saw to the lamp. Finally she just stood
in the middle of the floor with her hands clasped, looking in
front of her and listening to the noise all around her.

"Silly little thing, decking herself out in white," she
heard someone say behind her. Then she went over and
sat by Jonas, and as she sat down she burst into tears.

But she wasn't really crying, the tears ran so gently and
quietly down her cheeks. No one noticed them except
Jonas. He got really frightened; he patted her and took
her hand, holding it tenderly in his, asking over and over
again what was wrong and why she was crying. Then she
looked at him so warmly and smiled so sweetly, as she
always did when they spoke to each other.

"It's nothing, Jonas dear, it's only tears of joy."

Then he was reassured, because he could see that it was
true.

"Dear Jonas," she said then, "we'll go upstairs now."

And so they did. They said good-bye to everybody,
happily and affectionately, like the bridal pair they were,
and went up to their room.

It had all been got ready just as Frida had arranged,
the bed nicely made up with the sheets with lace insertions,
the widest in the shop; there were fresh-cut flowers on the
table, and a clean white cloth with hemstitching, and the
same on the chest of drawers. The window was open to
the silence of the late summer night with its clear stars
shining in.

How quiet and peaceful it was here. They threw their arms around each other, overwhelmed with bliss. They stood there, entirely filled with their happiness, for a long while, so long that they were not aware of time. Downstairs the noise went on, but it was strange how they didn't hear it. It was strange not being able to hear anything like that, anything at all.

They undressed and got into bed, caressing each other and whispering. They thrilled to each other, and felt the most wonderful feeling that they had never known before, which was like nothing else—nothing.

She had never thought that love could be so great. She had thought a lot about all this, but had never really been able to imagine it. It was as though she had lived her life just for this moment when she and Jonas became one. He held her in his arms, strong from all he had carried in his life, and she gave herself to her beloved; it was so unspeakably lovely to give him all she had, so really wonderful. She bit him with her false teeth so that he was quite dizzy. She, too, felt a little stupefied soon afterwards, but it was love speaking, that great, divine love, the incomprehensible miracle which made everything sacred.

Afterwards they lay side by side, tired and blissful, just holding each other's hand, as though that were even more tender than being caressed. They were almost numbed by the perfection of their happiness.

Jonas fell asleep, replete with his day. He was so handsome and good as he lay there beside her on the pillow; she stroked his hair and arranged it. She, too, felt a little exhausted, but she lay listening in the semi-darkness with open eyes.

How quiet it was, how extraordinarily quiet. Were they still there, or had they gone? She heard nothing but the great, unfathomable night, and the loved one at her side, snoring softly. Otherwise nothing.

She crept down beside him and she, too, fell asleep, his

hand tightly clasped in hers. They lay there together in the darkness, near each other, with burning cheeks and their mouths half-open for a kiss. And like a heavenly song of praise, like a hosanna of light around the only living thing, the stars rose around their bed in mighty hosts, their numbers increasing with the darkness.

Father and I

WHEN I was getting on toward ten, I remember, Father took me by the hand one Sunday afternoon, as we were to go out into the woods and listen to the birds singing. Waving good-bye to Mother, who had to stay at home and get the evening meal, we set off briskly in the warm sunshine. We didn't make any great to-do about this going to listen to the birds, as though it were something extra special or wonderful; we were sound, sensible people, Father and I, brought up with nature and used to it. There was nothing to make a fuss about. It was just that it was Sunday afternoon and Father was free. We walked along the railway line, where people were not allowed to go as a rule, but Father worked on the railway and so he had a right to. By doing this we could get straight into the woods, too, without going a round-about way.

Soon the bird song began and all the rest. There was a twittering of finches and willow warblers, thrushes and sparrows in the bushes, the hum that goes on all around you as soon as you enter a wood. The ground was white with wood anemones, the birches had just come out into leaf, and the spruces had fresh shoots; there were scents on all sides, and underfoot the mossy earth lay steaming in the sun. There was noise and movement everywhere; bumble-bees came out of their holes, midges swarmed wherever it was marshy, and birds darted out of the bushes to catch them and back again as quickly.

All at once a train came rushing along and we had to go down on to the embankment. Father hailed the engine driver with two fingers to his Sunday hat and the driver saluted and extended his hand. It all happened quickly;

then on we went, taking big strides so as to tread on the sleepers and not in the gravel, which was heavy going and rough on the shoes. The sleepers sweated tar in the heat, everything smelled, grease and meadowsweet, tar and heather by turns. The rails glinted in the sun. On either side of the line were telegraph poles, which sang as you passed them. Yes, it was a lovely day. The sky was quite clear, not a cloud to be seen, and there couldn't be any, either, on a day like this, from what Father said.

After a while we came to a field of oats to the right of the line, where a crofter we knew had a clearing. The oats had come up close and even. Father scanned them with an expert eye and I could see he was satisfied. I knew very little about such things, having been born in a town. Then we came to the bridge over a stream, which most of the time had no water to speak of but which now was in full spate. We held hands so as not to fall down between the sleepers. After that it is not long before you come to the platelayer's cottage lying embedded in greenery, apple trees and gooseberry bushes. We called in to see them and were offered milk, and saw their pig and hens and fruit trees in blossom; then we went on. We wanted to get to the river, for it was more beautiful there than anywhere else; there was something special about it, as farther upstream it flowed past where Father had lived as a child. We usually liked to come as far as this before we turned back, and today, too, we got there after a good walk. It was near the next station, but we didn't go so far. Father just looked to see that the semaphore was right—he thought of everything.

We stopped by the river, which murmured in the hot sun, broad and friendly. The shady trees hung along the banks and were reflected in the backwater. It was all fresh and light here; a soft breeze was blowing off the small lakes higher up. We climbed down the slope and walked a little way along the bank, Father pointing out the spots for fishing. He had sat here on the stones as a boy, waiting for perch all day long; often there wasn't even a bite, but it was a blissful life. Now he didn't have time. We hung about on the bank for a good while, making a noise, pushing out bits of bark for the current to take, throwing pebbles out into the water to see who could throw farthest; we were both gay and cheerful by nature, Father and I. At last we felt tired and that we had had enough, and we set off for home.

It was beginning to get dark. The woods were changed— it wasn't dark there yet, but almost. We quickened our steps. Mother would be getting anxious and waiting with supper. She was always afraid something was going to happen. But it hadn't; it had been a lovely day, nothing had happened that shouldn't. We were content with everything.

The twilight deepened. The trees were so funny. They stood listening to every step we took, as if they didn't know who we were. Under one of them was a glow-worm. It lay down there in the dark staring at us. I squeezed Father's hand, but he didn't see the strange glow, just walked on. Now it was quite dark. We came to the bridge over the stream. It roared down there in the depths, horribly, as though it wanted to swallow us up; the abyss yawned below us. We trod carefully on the sleepers, holding each other tightly by the hand so as not to fall in. I thought Father would carry me across, but he didn't say anything; he probably wanted me to be like him and think nothing of it.

We went on. Father was so calm as he walked there in the darkness, with even strides, not speaking, thinking to himself. I couldn't understand how he could be so calm when it was so murky. I looked all around me in fear. Nothing but darkness everywhere. I hardly dared take a deep breath, for then you got so much darkness inside you, and that was dangerous. I thought it meant you would soon die. I remember quite well that's what I thought then. The embankment sloped steeply down, as though into chasms black as night. The telegraph poles rose, ghostly, to the sky. Inside them was a hollow rumble, as though someone were talking deep down in the earth and the white porcelain caps sat huddled fearfully together listening to it. It was all horrible. Nothing was right, nothing real; it was all so weird.

Hugging close to Father, I whispered, "Father, why is it so horrible when it's dark?"

"No, my boy, it's not horrible," he said, taking me by the hand.

"Yes, Father, it is."

"No, my child, you mustn't think that. Not when we know there is a God."

I felt so lonely, forsaken. It was so strange that only I was afraid, not Father, that we didn't think the same. And strange that what he said didn't help me and stop me from being afraid. Not even what he said about God helped me. I thought he too was horrible. It was horrible that he was everywhere here in the darkness, down under the trees, in the telegraph poles which rumbled—that must be he— everywhere. And yet you could never see him.

We walked in silence, each with his own thoughts. My heart contracted, as though the darkness had got in and was beginning to squeeze it.

Then, as we were rounding a bend, we suddenly heard a mighty roar behind us! We were awakened out of our thoughts in alarm. Father pulled me down on to the embankment, down into the abyss, held me there. Then the train tore past, a black train. All the lights in the carriages were out, and it was going at frantic speed. What sort of train was it? There wasn't one due now! We gazed at it in terror. The fire blazed in the huge engine as they shovelled in coal; sparks whirled out into the night. It was terrible. The driver stood there in the light of the fire, pale, motionless, his features as though turned to stone. Father didn't recognize him, didn't know who he was. The man just stared straight ahead, as though intent only on rushing into the darkness, far into the darkness that had no end.

Beside myself with dread, I stood there panting, gazing after the furious vision. It was swallowed up by the night. Father took me up on to the line; we hurried home. He said, "Strange, what train was that? And I didn't recognize the driver." Then we walked on in silence.

But my whole body was shaking. It was for me, for my sake. I sensed what it meant: it was the anguish that was to come, the unknown, all that Father knew nothing about, that he wouldn't be able to protect me against. That was how this world, this life, would be for me; not like Father's, where everything was secure and certain. It wasn't a real world, a real life. It just hurtled, blazing, into the darkness that had no end.

The Adventure

A SHIP with black sails came to take me away. And I went on board willingly enough. I might just as well take a little trip; I was young and carefree and had a longing for the sea. We put out from the coast, which soon disappeared behind us, and the ship was borne steadily along by a fresh wind. Those of the crew with whom I came in contact were stern and grave; we had little to say to each other on board. We sailed and sailed day and night for a long time and on the same course. We did not come across any land. We sailed on year after year; the sea was blank, the wind good. There was no sign of land. At last I thought this was strange and asked one of the crew what was the reason. He answered that there was no world any longer. It was annihilated, had sunk down into the depths. There was only ourselves.

I thought that was exciting. We kept on sailing for a long time. The sea lay void. The wind filled the black sails. Everything was empty; there were only the depths below us. Then a frightful storm burst. The sea roared and heaved all around us. We fought in the darkness. The storm did not cease, nor the darkness. Year after year it continued. The clouds trailed across the black sails; everything was black and empty and desolate. We fought in the night, in anguish and need, wrought-up, lacerated, without daring to hope any more.

Then at last we heard the deafening roar of breakers. We were cast by a mighty wave against a rocky island which rose out of the sea. The ship was broken to pieces; we clung to the rock. The wreckage and shreds of sail floated about; we clung fast to the ground. At long last it grew light and we could see. The little island on which we had been saved was rugged and dark. There was only a single storm-blown tree, no flowers or verdure. We clung fast. We were happy. We laid our cheeks to the ground and wept for joy. It was the world beginning to rise up out of the depths again.

A Hero's Death

IN a town where the people never seemed to get enough
amusement a committee had engaged a man who was to
balance on his head up on the church spire and then fall
down and kill himself. He was to have 500,000 for doing it.
In all levels of society, all spheres, there was keen interest
in this undertaking; the tickets were snapped up in a few
days and it was the sole topic of conversation. Everyone
thought it was a very daring thing to do. But then, of
course, the price was in keeping. It was none too pleasant
to fall and kill yourself, and from such a height too. But it
was also admitted that it was a handsome fee. The syndicate
which had arranged everything had certainly not spared
itself in any way and people were proud that it had been
possible to form one like it in the town. Naturally, attention
was also riveted on the man who had undertaken to per-
form the feat. The interviewers from the press fell on him
with gusto, for there were only a few days left until the
performance was to take place. He received them affably
in his suite at the town's most fashionable hotel.

"Well, for me it's all a matter of business," he said. "I
have been offered the sum known to you, and I have
accepted the offer. That is all."

"But don't you think it's unpleasant having to lose your
life? We realize the necessity, of course; otherwise it
wouldn't be much of a sensation and the syndicate couldn't
pay as it has done, but it can't be too nice for you."

"No, you're right there, and the thought has occurred to
me, too. But one does anything for money."

On the basis of these statements long articles were
written in the newspapers about the hitherto unknown

man, about his past, his views, his attitude to various problems of the day, his character and private person. His picture was in every paper one opened. It showed a strong young man. There was nothing remarkable about him, but he looked spirited and healthy and had a frank, vigorous face; a typical representative of the best youth of the age, willing and sound. It was studied in all the cafés, while people made ready for the coming sensation. There was nothing wrong about it, they thought; a nice young man, the women thought he was wonderful. Those who had more sense shrugged their shoulders; smart bit of work, they said. All were unanimous on one thing, however: that the idea was strange and fantastic and that this sort of thing could only have occurred in our remarkable age with its flurry and intensity and its faculty of sacrificing all. And it was agreed that the syndicate deserved every praise for not having cavilled at expense when it came to arranging something like this and really giving the town a chance to witness such a spectacle. It would no doubt cover its expenditure by the high price of the tickets, but it took the risk at any rate.

At last the great day arrived. The space around the church was packed with people. The excitement was intense. All held their breath, in a frenzy of expectation at what was going to happen.

And the man fell; it was soon over. The people shuddered, then got up to go home. In a way they felt a certain disappointment. It had been splendid, but . . . He had only fallen and killed himself after all. It was a lot of money to pay for something that was so simple. Of course he had been frightfully mutilated, but what was the good of that? A promising young man sacrificed in that way. People went home disgruntled; the women put up their sunshades. No, awful things like that really ought to be forbidden. What pleasure did it give anyone? On second thought the whole thing was disgraceful.

The Venerated Bones

TWO nations had waged a great war together. They were both very proud of it and it still kept passions alive compared to which the ordinary small human ones were nothing. The people who were left abandoned themselves to them with fanatic zeal. On both sides of the frontier, where the battle had raged backward and forward and the combatants had been hideously mutilated, huge memorials had been erected to the fallen who had sacrificed themselves for their country and now rested here in its earth. The nations made pilgrimages there, each to their own, and the crowds were harangued with glowing words about the heroes whose bones slept under the soil, hallowed by a heroic death, vested with honour for evermore.

Then a horrible rumour got about among the two nations concerning something that was supposed to happen out there on the old battlefields at night. They were haunted. The dead rose up out of their graves and crossed the frontier, sought each other out, as if they were reconciled.

Everyone heard of this with deep resentment. The fallen heroes, those who were revered by the entire nation, they sought out the enemy, became reconciled with him! It was appalling.

Both nations sent out a commission to investigate the matter. The members lay in wait behind one or two withered trees that were still standing, and waited for midnight.

Ghastly, it was actually true! Horrible shapes rose out of the arid ground and went in the direction of the frontier;

they seemed to be carrying something. The commission hurried toward them, full of indignation.

"What, you who have sacrificed yourselves for your country, you whom we revere above all, to whom we pilgrimage in order to venerate and remember you, whose resting-place we hold sacred, you fraternize with the enemy! You reconcile yourselves with him!"

The fallen heroes looked at the commission in astonishment. "By no means. We hate each other as much as ever. We are only exchanging bones, everything is in such a muddle."

Saviour John

MY name is John, but I am called the Saviour, because I am to save mankind on earth. I am the one chosen for this and that is why I am so called. I am not like other people; no one here in the town is like me. The Lord has kindled a fire in my breast which never goes out; I can always feel it burning and burning inside, day and night. I feel that I must save them, that I am to be sacrificed for their sake. Through my faith, which I preach to them, they shall be redeemed.

Yes, I feel I must believe—must believe for them. For all who doubt, for all who hunger and thirst and cannot be satisfied. I shall refresh them. In their anguish and need they call to me, and I wipe out everything as with a gentle and merciful hand, and it is no more.

Yes, I am to save mankind on earth. From the age of fourteen I have known that I am chosen for it. Since then I have been different from all others.

I don't dress like other people either—you can tell just from that. I have two rows of silver buttons on my jacket and a green band around my waist, and a red one around my arm. On a string around my neck I wear the lid of a cigar box with the picture of a pretty young woman on it; I can't remember now what it means. That's how I am dressed. But fastened by an invisible thread around my forehead I wear a star which I have cut out of tin. It gleams and sparkles in the sun. It can be seen from afar and it shines so that no one can help noticing it.

When I walk down the street everyone stares after me in wonder. Look at the Saviour, they say to each other. For they know that's who I am. They know I have come to save them.

But they don't understand me yet. They don't believe as they should. Not as *I* believe. There is no fire inside them, not as with me. That is why I must speak to them, teach them to believe; that is why I must stay here for a long time yet.

I think it is so strange—they see their Saviour and hear his voice, he is right among them, and still they do not understand him. But in time to come their eyes will be opened and they will see him as he is.

Market today. Been up to the market place and preached as usual. The farmers were there with their carts. All gathered around me. I spoke of everything that I bear within me, of my message which I shall proclaim to the whole world: that I am come to redeem them, that through me they shall gain peace. They listened attentively; I think they were comforted by my words.

I don't understand why they laugh. I myself never laugh. For me everything is serious. As I stood there looking out over the large crowd of people and thinking that in each one of them there was a soul that must be saved if it was not to go under, that must believe if it was not to plunge into despair, I was moved by such solemnity and earnestness. Oh, it was glorious to stand like that and feel them gathered around me. I seemed for a moment to be looking out over countless multitudes, even all those who had not come to hear me today—for it is quite a small market and there are not so many people; to be looking out over all the people on earth, and all hungered and thirsted for peace, and I was to save them. It was a blissful moment. I shall never forget it.

I think I was filled with the spirit today and that they understood me.

When I had finished, one of them stepped forward and gave me a cabbage on behalf of everyone there. I brought it home and this evening I have made good, nourishing soup from it. It is a long time since I have had anything hot to eat. God bless him.

Oh, the pity of humanity. They are all unhappy, distressed; they all suffer. Johansson, the baker, is unhappy because they no longer buy his bread now that a bakery has opened next door. His bread is so good too; he has often given me a loaf to take home. All bread is good. Ekström, the policeman, whom I often talk to, is unhappy because his wife neglects the house, and I don't think she bothers about him any more. Even the magistrate is unhappy, because he has lost his only son.

Only I am happy. For in me burns the fire of faith which can never go out, which shall burn and burn until it has consumed me. I have no uneasiness, no anxiety; I am not like them. That would not be right.

No, I must not despair. I must believe for them.

They have taken me to the workhouse so that I shall be free of all earthly worries and can devote myself entirely to my mission as Saviour. I am well off here; we get food twice a day. The others here are poor people. I feel so sorry for them. They are quiet, good souls; I don't think anyone has ever understood me so well as they do. They call me the Saviour, like everyone else, and have great respect for me.

In the evenings I preach to them. They listen devoutly, and every word reaches their hearts. How their eyes shine when I speak! They cling to me—to my words—as their only hope. Yes, they know that I have come to save them.

Always after supper I gather them around me like this

and speak full of rapture, full of the heavenly light within me; speak of the faith that can overcome everything, that transforms this world to a happy home given us by the Highest. The superintendent says that I may, by all means —it doesn't matter. He is pleased with me. Then we go to rest. There are four of us in our room. The star hangs over my bed; it shines and burns all night long in the dark above me. It casts its light over my face as I sleep. I am not like the others on earth.

Oh, terrifying anguish in my soul! Anguish, despair fills us all.

The star is missing, the star of salvation which alone can guide us aright. This morning when I woke up, the nail I hang it on was empty. No one knows where it has gone. Darkness surrounds us. I look for a single ray of light but find none, no way out of the terrible darkness. All are broken-hearted, the whole town is sunk in grief. From up here at the workhouse we can see it lying like ashes. The sky is grey and leaden, there is no sign of light.

How are we to be saved from our need? How are we to find the way out of the despair that seizes us?

All put their hope in me. But what am I if the star does not shine above my head, if the heavenly light does not lead me? I am nothing then; I am just as poor as all the others.

Who is to save us then?

Now it has been found. All day I have thanked and praised on my knees.

Old Enok had taken it. We found it under his mattress. Now we are all glad and undismayed once more. My faith glows stronger than ever after this trial I have undergone.

He had only done it as a joke. I have forgiven him.

Sometimes I feel such loneliness and emptiness round me. It seems as if people do not understand my message to

them. I doubt my power over their souls. How can I
redeem them?

They always smile so when I speak. As soon as they see
me their faces light up. But do they really believe in me?

I think it is so strange that they do not understand who I
am, that they cannot feel the fire which burns inside me—
my heavenly rapture—how everything glows and is consumed within me. I can feel it myself so well.

Sometimes when I preach, it is as if I were alone,
although there are large crowds listening all around me.
I am like a flame leaping higher and higher, rising clearer
and purer toward the sky. But no one warms himself at it.

O doubt, that is trying to crush me! What makes us so
poor and abased as you do?

Today I have been out with the flowers and the birds.
They were so glad because I came. The larks rejoiced;
primroses and violets peeped up everywhere out of the
grass. I preached for a while in the deepest reverence.
Everything listened. The larks stopped above my head to
hear me. What peace the soul feels in the country; everything there understands me so well!

If people were flowers and trees, then they would
understand me too. Yes, they would be much happier
then.

They are bound to the earth and yet do not belong to it.
They are flowers plucked up by the roots. The sun only
burns them; the soil is just waiting for them to become soil.
Nothing here makes them happy; nothing can save them
except the message from heaven which I want to bring
them. Then everything will be explained and the earth
will smell of lilies. Then they will gain peace.

When I came back to the town in the evening, there
were a lot of people collected outside the taverns and they
called for their Saviour, wanted me to preach to them.
But I said that I had been away talking to my God and that
I must go home and think over what he had said.

Perhaps that was not right. But I felt like a stranger and went home grieving.

O my heart, how hard it is to live! How heavy to bear is the calling that has been laid upon me!

This afternoon as I walked along the street deep in thought, I found myself in the midst of the children who were coming from school. They flocked around me.

"Look at the Saviour," they cried, "look at the Saviour!"

They pressed around from all sides; I had to stop.

Then one of them stretched up his arms and shouted, "Crucified! Crucified!"

I think someone had taught it to them, for with one accord they all did the same.

They stretched up their small hands and all around me their childish voices shouted, "Crucified! Crucified!"

It was as if a sword had pierced my breast. I felt my heart stand still; the sweat of anguish broke out on my brow. With their shouting and noise in my ears I forced my way through them and escaped. I went into the yard of Lundgren, the carpenter, and wept.

I love children. No one loves them as I do. When I look into their bright eyes I feel a joy which nothing else on earth can give. I want them to come to me. Then I would pick them up on my knee and stroke their hair and they would lay their warm little cheeks against mine. . . .

I have often see Johansson the baker's little boy do that when Johansson has sat down to rest in the evening. I have seen him pat his father's cheek and put his arms around his neck and they have sat like that for a long time without a thought for anything else. It has made me long for a little hand to pat me like that. . . .

But he who is to save mankind walks alone among them like a stranger. He has no home here, no joy, no sorrow that belongs to the earth. He is an outcast, for in him burns the fire that is to consume them. Who is not as they are? Crucified! Crucified!

Just believe and believe. Believe for them all. Oh, every evening I am as tired as though I had lived their thousand lives. I collapse on my bed and fall asleep like an animal. Only the star burns above my weary body so that I shall waken again and believe still more.

Why have I been chosen for it? Often as I sit at the window up here at the workhouse and look out over the town, I think it is so strange that I of all people shall save them. I am so lowly; many have greater power and might on earth than I. The calling weighs me down like a burden which I am too weak to bear. I want to sink down on my knees. My soul is filled with such anguish. . . .

Their Saviour surely must not sink down. *He* must not feel anguish in his soul.

Oh, why must I, who am weakest of all, believe for them?

This afternoon as I was walking across the market place, I met the magistrate. As he passed he nodded kindly. "Good afternoon, John," he said.

I almost stopped short. . . .

He did not call me the Saviour!

"Good afternoon, John," was all he said. Just John, nothing else.

No one has called me that since I was a child. Now I remember, it was my mother who called me that. She would pick me up on her knee and stroke my head. I remember it so well now that I think back. . . .

Good afternoon, John. . . .

She was so good to me. In the evenings she would come home and light the lamp and prepare the food, and then I would creep up on her knee. Her hair was quite golden, her hands nice and white from scrubbing floors all day. Now I remember it all so well—it is her I carry around my neck, it is Mother.

Good afternoon, John. . . .

How nice it felt when he said that. So nice and safe. All seemed to grow quite still inside me, no worry, no fear of anything.

Just John, nothing else.

Oh, if only I could be like all the others! If I could take off the sign of my Saviour's calling and go about like one of them; just be as they are. Live here quietly and peacefully with my earthly work, as the others do, day after day; and in the evening go to bed tired from worldly tasks, which I have done as I should, not from believing, just believing. . . .

Perhaps I could be a turner at Lundgren the carpenter's. Or, if that was difficult, then I could sweep the yard.

And so I would be like them. And there would not be this fire burning in me any more! No anguish would consume me any more.

Just John, nothing else. . . . They would all know so well who I was, would see me every day going about my business. John, he's the one who sweeps the yard. . . .

Oh, why must I save them, I who am the poorest and weakest of all? I who want to live here in peace, so grateful for the earth which has bidden me here to it. Like a guest, sunk down on his knees at the rich table; like a flower that scarcely raises itself above the ground.

O God, my Father, if it be possible, then let this cup pass from me!

No, no! I must not doubt! Not fail them!

What is it that wants to lead my soul astray? What is it

that wants to hurl them all down into an abyss of darkness, because I fail them?

Something terrible has happened to me! What is it? Do I not believe any more?

Yes, yes! I believe! I believe as never before. I shall save them. It is *I*, it is *I* who will save them.

I walk and walk here at night, have no peace. In the streets, out on the roads, far into the woods and back again. There is a wind, the clouds are driving before it. Where am I—my head is burning—I am so tired. . . .

Yes, I believe! I believe! I shall save them, I shall be sacrificed for them. Soon, soon. . . .

Why, then, do I feel such anguish? Surely the Saviour of mankind must not fear and despair as I do?

No, no. . . .

Am I out in the woods again? Don't I hear the trees soughing? Why am I wandering about here? Why am I not with the people who are waiting and waiting? . . .

But they don't understand me!

How are they to understand me when I am nothing but despair and torment? How are they to believe in me when I wander about in the darkness without peace?

I cannot save them! It is not I, not I!

Yes, their Saviour is all the anguish and need that they do not understand. He is like a bird crying in the sky far above their heads. They hear his cries up there but think it is not for them, because he is floating so high. Not until he falls dead and bleeding to earth do they understand him. Only then can they believe.

Crucified! Crucified!

Yes, I want to be sacrificed, I want to be sacrificed!

They shall be redeemed by my blood, by my poor blood. Soon, soon it will happen. . . .

Sleep sweetly all small flowers here in the darkness, all meadows, all trees, all people in the world. Have peace, dear earth. I shall redeem you.

I watch over you in the night. All your anguish is mine. You shall not suffer, not be troubled about anything. I shall lay down my life for you.

How silent it is here in the wood! Am I walking on dead leaves? My footsteps make no sound.

Many flowers and leaves are mouldering now in the autumn and it is so soft under the trees, silent and soft. There is a smell of earth.

Is that the clock striking in the town? One—two—

Oh, I am so tired, so tired—I want to go home.

I must go home now and rest, lie down for a while. They will be wondering where I am.

I must be coming out on to the road now. It is muddy— I think it rained yesterday—how windy it is!

No, it is the bell ringing and ringing! It booms in the air. What is it? It sounds terrible. There are a lot of them, they are tolling and booming as though for Judgment Day! What is it? I must run!

Fire! Fire! The flames are leaping up, the sky is blood red! The town is on fire! The world is on fire, it is perishing!

O God, I must save them! I must save them. They are waiting for me—isn't he coming, isn't he coming. . . .

Yes, I'm running, I'm running. I am coming to save them. It's the mud clinging to me. I'm running!

Heaven and earth are on fire! They are crashing down. Like a sea of fire. I must save them, I must save them!

My heart, you must not pain me—good heart, don't pain me so, I cannot run then, cannot breathe—and I must save them! You know that I must save them.

Nothing but a blazing sea! And the storm rages. Heaven is driving in flames across the world and setting it alight.

Now, now the others are beside me. They are running in the same direction as I.

"The world is perishing," I shout at them.

"Oh," they reply, "it's only the workhouse."

Yes, it's the workhouse! All those poor people, those who

hunger and thirst because they cannot believe, they're burning to death! They are perishing! Only I can save them!

My heart, do not hurt so; we are nearly there—soon, soon. . . .

The flames leap up, the smoke is here in the street, I can feel the heat. . . .

Now I am there.

The superintendent—a lot of people have collected here. "I shall save them, I shall save them!" I shout.

"There's no one there to save!" they call, placing themselves in the way. They don't understand me. I rush into the flames.

The heat almost stuns me. No, I do not sink down— their Saviour must not sink down. I only stagger at first —grope my way forward—through the hall—into the rooms. . . .

It is empty here—they are upstairs. . . .

The smoke nearly stifles me on the stairs. No, no, I do not sink down. I shall save them—all—all. . . .

Where are they?

I grope my way forward in a daze. The smoke is thick— the flames leap up—I lurch about. . . .

Where are they?

Old Man Enok who cannot manage by himself—and Anton whose legs are paralysed—and old Kristina who is out of her wits—and Samuelsson—and Manfred from the gaol. . . .

I can't find them. . . .

I creep along the floor. The flames lick after me. There is a crackling all around me—a roar—it's collapsing. . . . Where are they? They have moved the furniture out, the beds, the chairs. . . . It's bare and empty—as though nobody lived here. Where are they? They can't be here— only I—only I. . . .

It's on fire! On fire! The beams crash down. The flames

leap up everywhere. I rush around. Where are they—where are they? All the poor—I can't find them—they're not here. . . . Only fire and devastation—only I—only I. . . .

O my heart, is it you that is burning? Perhaps it's only you. I can feel you consuming my body, my breast, my limbs, until nothing is left but you! Yes, consume it, consume it! I want only to be you, only you, heart that hungers and thirsts, only you, fire that devours me!

Nothing else—nothing else—only you. . . .

No—I can't go on any—any longer. . . . It's the end. . . . Yes, yes, I sink down—it's the end—end. . . .

O God, forgive me for not finding the people I was to save. I can't find them. Forgive a heart that's on fire—only with longing to be sacrificed—to die—to die. . . .

Yes, I feel that you forgive me. You forgive the heart that burns for you—you love it—yes, you love it. You let it be consumed—consumed—you let it have peace—peace. . . .

Crucified! Crucified!

The Experimental World

ONCE upon a time there was a world which was not intended to be a real, proper world but which was only meant to experiment with this and that, where one could see by trial and error how everything turned out, what could be made of it. It was to be like a laboratory, a research station where various suggestions and ideas could be tried out to see what they were worth. If anything chanced to give a satisfactory result, proved to be perfect, then it was to be used elsewhere.

A start was made with a little of everything. Plants and trees were set out and tended, fertilized with sun. They grew a bit, then they died out and mouldered away, others had to be started. Many animals were tried, they did fairly well, they developed; but then all at once they stopped where they were or crept back almost to where they had begun; everything came to a standstill. But it didn't matter very much; failures were only to be expected. Some things were not so bad for all that, and much was learned.

Then it was seen what could be done with human beings. It didn't go at all well. They grew a bit, but then they slipped back again. They could be got so that they seemed almost perfect, whole nations, great and noble, but all at once they slipped back, proved to be nothing but animals. But it didn't matter very much; failures were only to be expected. The earth was full of bones from all kinds of human beings who had turned out badly, from nations that had been a failure. But quite a lot was learned about how it should not be.

Then came the idea to try just one or two; it was no use

with such a lot of people. A boy- and a girl-child were chosen who were to grow up in the most beautiful part of the earth. They were allowed to run about in the woods and romp, play under the trees and take delight in everything. They were allowed to become a young man and woman who loved one another, their happiness was complete, their eyes met as openly as if their love had been but a clear summer's day. Even all the human failures around them saw that there was an unaccountable splendour about them which made them different from everything else in the world. And they rejoiced at it; they could do that at least. Love drew the two lovers together. It could not remain merely as a beautiful earthly day; it rose up into a light where the young people felt dizzy, where they had to shut their eyes or be blinded; their hearts thumped, their lips quivered. They lay under the rose trees in the most beautiful part of the earth, in a wonderful night which had been provided for them. And they fell asleep in bliss, in the ecstasy and perfect beauty of love, locked in each other's arms. They awakened no more; they were dead. They were to be used elsewhere.

The Lift That Went Down into Hell

MR SMITH, a prosperous businessman, opened the elegant hotel lift and amorously handed in a gracile creature smelling of furs and powder. They nestled together on the soft seat and the lift started downward. The little lady extended her half-open mouth, which was moist with wine, and they kissed. They had dined up on the terrace, under the stars; now they were going out to amuse themselves.

"Darling, how divine it was up there," she whispered. "So poetic sitting there with you, like being up among the stars. That's when you really know what love is. You do love me, don't you?"

Mr Smith answered with a kiss that lasted still longer; the lift went down.

"A good thing you came, my darling," he said; "otherwise I'd have been in an awful state."

"Yes, but you can just imagine how insufferable he was. The second I started getting ready he asked where I was going. 'I'll go where I please,' I said. 'I'm no prisoner.' Then he deliberately sat and stared at me the whole time I was changing, putting on my new beige—do you think it's becoming? What do you think looks best, by the way, perhaps pink after all?"

"Everything becomes you, darling," the man said, "but I've never seen you so lovely as this evening."

She opened her fur coat with a gratified smile, they kissed for a long time, the lift went down.

"Then when I was ready to go he took my hand and squeezed it so that it still hurts, and didn't say a word. He's so brutal, you've no idea! 'Well, good-bye,' I said. But not a word from him. He's so unreasonable, so frightfully, I can't stand it."

"Poor little thing," said Mr Smith.

"As though I can't go out for a bit and enjoy myself. But then he's so deadly serious, you've no idea. He can't take anything simply and naturally. It's as though it were a matter of life and death the whole time."

"Poor pet, what you must have gone through."

"Oh, I've suffered terribly. No one has suffered as I have. Not until I met you did I know what love is."

"Sweetheart," Smith said, hugging her; the lift went down.

"Fancy," she said, when she had got her breath after the embrace, "sitting with you up there gazing at the stars and dreaming—oh, I'll never forget it. You see, the thing is—Arvid is impossible, he's so everlastingly solemn, he hasn't a scrap of poetry in him, he has no feeling for it."

"Darling, it's intolerable."

"Yes, isn't it—intolerable. But," she went on, giving him her hand with a smile, "let's not sit thinking of all that. We're out to enjoy ourselves. You do really love me?"

"Do I!" he said, bending her back so that she gasped; the lift went down. Leaning over her he fondled her; she blushed.

"Let us make love tonight—as never before. Hm?" he whispered.

She pressed him to her and closed her eyes; the lift went down.

Down and down it went.

At last Smith got to his feet, his face flushed.

"But what's the matter with the lift?" he exclaimed. "Why doesn't it stop? We've been sitting here for ever so long talking, haven't we?"

"Yes, darling, I suppose we have, time goes so quickly."

"Good Heavens, we've been sitting here for ages! What's the idea?"

He glanced out through the grill. Nothing but pitch darkness. And the lift went on and on at a good, even pace, deeper and deeper down.

"Heavens alive, what's the idea? It's like dropping down into an empty pit. And we've been doing this for God knows how long."

They tried to peep down into the abyss. It was pitch dark. They just sank and sank down into it.

"This is all going to hell," Smith said.

"Oh dear," the woman wailed, clinging to his arm, "I'm so nervous. You'll have to pull the emergency brake."

Smith pulled for all he was worth. It was no good. The lift merely plunged down and down interminably.

"It's frightful," she cried. "What are we going to do!"

"Yes, what the devil is one to do?" Smith said. "This is crazy."

The little lady was in despair and burst into tears.

"There, there, my sweet, don't cry, we must be sensible. There's nothing we can do. There now, sit down. That's right, now we'll sit here quietly both of us, close together, and see what happens. It must stop some time or there'll be the devil to pay."

They sat and waited.

"Just think of something like this happening," the woman said. "And we were going out to have fun."

"Yes, it's the very devil," Smith said.

"You do love me, don't you?"

"Darling," Smith said, putting his arms around her; the lift went down.

At last it stopped abruptly. There was such a bright light all around that it hurt the eyes. They were in hell. The Devil slid the grill aside politely.

"Good evening," he said with a deep bow. He was stylishly dressed in tails that hung on the hairy top vertebra as on a rusty nail.

Smith and the woman tottered out in a daze. "Where

in God's name are we?" they exclaimed, terrified by the weird apparition. The Devil, a shade embarrassed, enlightened them.

"But it's not as bad as it sounds," he hastened to add. "I hope you will have quite a pleasant time, I gather it's just for the night?"

"Yes, yes!" Smith assented eagerly, "it's just for the night. We're not going to stay, oh no!"

The little lady clung tremblingly to his arm. The light was so corrosive and yellowy green that they could hardly see, and there was a hot smell, they thought. When they had grown a little more used to it they discovered they were standing as it were in a square, around which houses with glowing doorways towered up in the darkness; the curtains were drawn but they could see through the chinks that something was burning inside.

"You are the two who love each other?" the Devil inquired.

"Yes, madly," the lady answered, giving him a look with her lovely eyes.

"Then this is the way," he said, and asked them to follow please. They slunk into a murky side street leading out of the square. An old cracked lantern was hanging outside a filthy, grease-stained doorway.

"Here it is." He opened the door and retired discreetly.

They went in. A new devil, fat, fawning, with large breasts and purple powder caked on the moustache around her mouth, received them. She smiled wheezily, a good-natured, knowing look in her beady eyes; around the horns in her forehead she had twined tufts of hair and fastened them with small blue silk ribbons.

"Oh, is it Mr Smith and the little lady?" she said. "It's in number eight then." And she gave them a large key.

They climbed the dim, greasy staircase. The stairs were slippery with fat; it was two flights up. Smith found number eight and went in. It was a fairly large, musty room. In the middle was a table with a grubby cloth; by the wall a bed with smoothed-down sheets. They thought it all very nice. They took off their coats and kissed for a long time.

A man came in unobtrusively from another door. He was dressed like a waiter but his dinner jacket was well cut and his shirtfront so clean that it gleamed ghostlike in the semi-darkness. He walked silently, his feet making no sound, and his movements were mechanical, unconscious almost. His features were stern, the eyes looking fixedly straight ahead. He was deathly pale; in one temple he had a bullet wound. He got the room ready, wiped the dressing-table, brought in a chamber-pot and a slop-pail.

They didn't take much notice of him, but as he was about to go, Smith said, "I think we'll have some wine. Bring us half a bottle of Madeira." The man bowed and disappeared.

Smith started getting undressed. The woman hesitated. "He's coming back," she said.

"Pshaw, in a place like this you needn't mind. Just take your things off." She got out of her dress, pulled up her panties coquettishly and sat on his knee. It was lovely.

"Just think," she whispered, "sitting here together, you and I, alone, in such a queer, romantic place. So poetic, I'll never forget it."

"Sweetheart," he said. They kissed for a long time.

The man came in again, soundlessly. Softly, mechanically, he put down the glasses, poured out the wine. The light from the table lamp fell on his face. There was nothing special about him except that he was deathly pale and had a bullet wound in his temple.

The woman leaped up with a scream.

"Oh my God! Arvid! Is it you? Is it you? Oh God in Heaven, he's dead! He's shot himself!"

The man stood motionless, just staring in front of him. His face showed no suffering; it was merely stern, very grave.

"But Arvid, what have you done, what have you done!
How could you! My dear, if I'd suspected anything like
that, you know I'd have stayed at home. But you never tell
me anything. You never said anything about it, not a
word! How was I to know when you never told me! Oh
my God. . . ."

Her whole body was shaking. The man looked at her as
at a stranger; his gaze was icy and grey, just went straight
through everything. The sallow face gleamed, no blood
came from the wound, there was just a hole there.

"Oh, it's ghastly, ghastly!" she cried. "I won't stay here!
Let's go at once. I can't stand it."

She grabbed her dress, hat and fur coat and rushed out,
followed by Smith. They slipped going down the stairs, she
sat down, got spittle and cigarette ash on her behind.
Downstairs the woman with the moustache was standing,
smiling good-naturedly and knowingly and nodding her
horns.

Out in the street they calmed down a little. The woman
put on her clothes, straightened herself, powdered her
nose. Smith put his arm protectingly round her waist,
kissed away the tears that were on the point of falling—he
was so good. They walked up into the square.

The head devil was walking about there, they ran into
him again. "You *have* been quick," he said. "I hope you've
been comfortable."

"Oh, it was dreadful," the lady said.

"No, don't say that, you can't think that. You should
have been here in the old days, it was different then. Hell
is nothing to complain of now. We do all we can not to
make it too obvious, on the contrary to make it enjoyable."

"Yes," Mr Smith said, "I must say it's a little more
humane anyway, that's true."

"Oh," the Devil said, "we've had everything modern-
ized, completely rearranged, as it should be."

"Yes, of course, you must keep up with the times."

"Yes, it's only the soul that suffers nowadays."

"Thank God for that," said the lady.

The Devil conducted them politely to the lift. "Good evening," he said with a deep bow, "welcome back." He shut the grill after them, the lift went up.

"Thank God that's over," they both said, relieved, and nestled up to one another on the seat.

"I should never have got through it without you," she whispered. He drew her to him, they kissed for a long time. "Fancy," she said, when she had got her breath after the embrace, "his doing such a thing! But he's always had such queer notions. He's never been able to take things simply and naturally, as they are. It's as though it were a matter of life and death the whole time."

"It's absurd," Smith said.

"He might have *told* me! Then I'd have stayed. We could have gone out another evening instead."

"Yes, of course," Smith said, "of course we could."

"But, darling, let's not sit thinking of that," she whispered, putting her arms around his neck. "It's over now."

"Yes, little darling, it's over now." He clasped her in his arms; the lift went up.

Love and Death

ONE evening as I was out walking with my sweetheart in the street, the door of a gloomy house we were passing was opened suddenly and a Cupid put one foot out of the darkness. He was no ordinary little Cupid, but a large man, heavy and muscular, with hair all over his body. He most resembled a brutish archer as he stood with his clumsy cross-bow and aimed at me. He shot an arrow which hit me in the breast; then he drew in his leg and shut the door of the house that was like a dark, cheerless fortress. I sank down; my sweetheart walked on. I don't think she noticed that I sank down. Had she noticed it she would certainly have stopped and bent over me and tried to do something for me. The fact that she walked on meant that she could not have seen it. My blood ran after her in the gutter for a while, but stopped when there was none left.

The Basement

W E have all seen him and see him nearly every day.
We don't take much notice of him. Now and then
we pass him as he lies there but pay little attention; it is as
though he should be here, as though he belonged to our
world. I mean Lindgren, the little old man with the
withered legs, the one who drags himself along the streets
and in the parks with the help of his hands. He wears
leather gloves; his legs, too, are covered with leather. The
short-bearded face is marked by suffering which it cannot
quite express; the eyes are small and submissive. We have
all met him, meet him continually. It is as though he were
a part of ourselves. In passing we put a coin in his worn-out
hand; he, too, must live.

But few know much about him other than that he exists.
So I am going to tell you a little more about the old man,
for I know him.

I had often stopped and talked to the old chap for a
while. There was something soothing and good about him
which I seemed to need. I had done this so often that
people must have thought he was an unfortunate relative
of mine. It is not so. There is no distress in our family; only
a grief which is ours and none other's, which we bear
erectly. But I felt I had to stand and talk to him sometimes:
for his sake, so that he would not feel like an outcast, but
also for my own, because he had something to tell me. And
there didn't seem to be any gulf between us. I often thought
that if I had not had any legs to walk with, had had to drag
myself along the ground as he did, it would not have suited
me so badly either. I should have had no reason to think
it strange that this had fallen to my lot. In this way there

was, after all, something we had in common.

One evening in the late autumn I came across him in a park where lovers used to meet. He was lying under a lamp in order to be seen, stretching out his worn hand though nobody came. No doubt he thought that love makes people generous. Actually he didn't know much about this world, but just lay stretching out his hand somewhere, just lived here all the same. It had been raining; he was muddy from the sodden ground and looked tired and ill.

"Hadn't you better be getting home, Lindgren?" I said. "It's late."

"Yes," he replied, "I suppose I had."

"I'll walk part of the way with you," I said. "Where do you live?"

He told me, we found that we lived not far from each other and went the same way.

We crossed a street.

"Isn't it risky," I asked, "when you want to get from one side to the other?"

"Oh no," he replied. "They're on the lookout for me. Yesterday a policeman stopped the entire traffic for me to cross. But he said I'd have to hurry, and you can't wonder. Oh no, everybody here knows me; they seem to think I belong here."

We went slowly on. I had to shorten my steps and even stop occasionally so that he could keep up. It started to drizzle. He shuffled along at my feet, the muddy hands scratching against the pavement, the body moving up and down. It was like an animal dragging itself home to its lair. Yet it was a human being like myself. I heard him talking and breathing down there as I was doing, but the street lamps shone feebly through the mist and I could hardly see him. I was filled with such pity as I heard him down there, struggling to keep up.

"Don't you think you have a hard lot to bear, Lindgren?" I said. "You must often feel it's unfair."

"No," he answered from below. "The odd thing is that it is not so bad as people think. You get used to it. And I was born with it; it's not as if a healthy grown man suddenly meets with something unexpected. No, I can't say I have anything to complain of, if I really come to think of it. There must be many who are worse off than I am. I am spared much that others have to go through. My life is quiet and secure; the world has been merciful to me. You must remember that I only come in contact with the good in it."

"Oh?" I said wonderingly.

"Yes, I only come in contact with good people; they're the only ones who stop and give me a coin. I know nothing about the others. They just walk past."

"Well, Lindgren, you know how to make the best of things," I answered with a smile.

"But it's true," he said seriously, "and it's something to be thankful for." I also took it seriously; in fact, realized that he was right. What a great blessing it was getting to know only the good in life!

We went on. Light was coming from a shop in a basement. "I'm going to buy bread here," he said, creeping up to the window and knocking. A girl came up with the parcel, which was all ready. "Good evening, Lindgren," she said. "Ugh, what weather! You ought to be getting home."

"Yes, I'm going," the old chap answered. They nodded good-bye to each other, and she closed the door after her.

"I always do my shopping in the basement," he said as we proceeded.

"Yes, I suppose so," I answered.

"People there are always so kind."

"Oh? Yes, perhaps."

"But they *are*," he said decidedly.

We struggled through one or two dark, hilly lanes.

"I live in the basement, too, as you can imagine," he

continued. "It suits me best. Our landlord arranged it. He is a remarkable man."

Then we went through one street after the other, groping our way along. It had never occurred to me that it was such a long way home. I felt tired, exhausted. It was as if I, too, were dragging myself along in the darkness, heavily and wearily, though I was no cripple. I walked erect, as one should walk. By the street lamps I saw him crawling down there; then he disappeared again. I merely heard his panting breath.

At last we turned into his street, and came up to the house where he lived. It was large and splendid; nearly all the windows were lighted. There seemed to be a party on the first floor. The chandeliers glistened, music penetrated out into the dismal autumn night and dancing couples could be seen flitting past. He crept forward to the three or four steps which led down to where he lived. Beside them was a window with a piece of curtain and a sardine tin with flower bulbs. "You'll come down, won't you, and have a look at my room?" he said.

I had not thought of that. I had not realized I would have to. I felt strangely heavy at heart. Why should I go down? We were not close enough friends to warrant it. I had come with him part of the way because we lived in much the same direction; I'd had no intention of going home with him. Why should I go down? But I had to.

It occurred to me that actually I knew the family up there who were giving the party. It was strange that they had not invited me; they must have forgotten.

"You don't mind my asking you down, do you?" the old chap asked, as though remarking on my silence.

"No," I said.

He had misunderstood me. I wanted to go down and see how he lived; that was why I had come along. I wanted to go where I was asked.

He shuffled down the steps, got out the key and put it in

the lock. I noticed that this had been moved lower down so that he could reach it.

"Our landlord had it done," he said. "He thinks of everything." The door opened and we went in. When the light had been put on I looked around the room. It was small and bare. The floor was cold stone with one or two bits of carpet on it. In the middle was a table which had part of the legs sawn off, and two low chairs. In one corner was the stove, which he could also use for cooking apparently. Beside it was a shelf that served as a pantry. The tins were arranged according to height, with labels on. Pieces of bread he had evidently saved for dipping in his coffee stood in a row. Around the shelf was a white, paper lace edging. At one end of the room was his bed, consisting of a bunk raised off the floor; the bedcover was clean and nice. Despite all the poverty, every corner of the room was neat and tidy. I don't know why, but this orderliness distressed me. Why did he have it like this? Had I been in his shoes I should have had it dirty and horrible—just a hole to creep into and hide, like an animal. It would have been easier then, I thought, to hold out. But it was clean and tidy everywhere.

It seemed a cosy little home as he crept about busily, reached up for the flower vase on the table and filled it with water, slid down again, got a cloth out of a little blue-painted chest, spread it, got out cups and saucers. It cut me to the heart to see him doing these homely things. He had taken off the leather gloves; his hands were flat with thick skin on the palms. He then lit the fire, blowing on it so that the flames roared up the pipe; added coal, took down the coffee-pot and put it on. I was not allowed to help him; no, he knew best how it should be. He did it all with such a deft and practised hand that you could see he enjoyed it, that he had grown fond of these little tasks. Now and then he would look up at me good-naturedly. There was something so warm and secure about him here in his home; he was not as he was in the street. Soon the coffee-pot was simmering on the fire and the aroma filled the room. When it was ready he crept up laboriously on to his chair and settled down, beaming and contented. He poured out the coffee and we began to drink. It was nice and warming. He thought I should eat some bread too, but I didn't want to take it from him. He himself ate with a marked solemnity, slowly breaking piece after piece and carefully picking up all the crumbs. There was such reverence about his meal. His eyes shone; never have I seen a face so radiant as his, never transfigured in such a tranquil way.

I felt at once moved and oppressed at seeing him like this in the midst of his affliction. How could he? I, who lived the real life, who merely sat here as a temporary guest in order to see what it was like down here in his lair—I had no peace. Well, I thought to myself, he probably has something else he hopes for. He must be one of those who believe in God and the like, and then anything can be endured, nothing is hard. And I remembered that I was going to ask him about this very thing, which forever weighed me down, which never gave me any peace, which dragged me down into the depths where I did not want to be. That was why I had come home with him, to ask him about it. I didn't belong down here, was only going to ask him about it.

"Tell me, Lindgren," I said, "when one's life is like yours, when one has to suffer as you do, I suppose one feels, more strongly than the rest of us, the need of believing that there is something outside this world, that there is a prevailing God who has a higher purpose with what he lays upon us?"

The old man pondered a moment.

"No," he replied slowly, "not when one's life can be like mine."

I thought this was strange, distressing to hear. Was he

not aware of his misery, did he not know how rich and glorious life should be?

"No," he said, lost in thought, "it is not we who need him. Even if he existed he could not tell us more than we already know and are grateful for.

"I have often talked to our landlord about it," he went on. "He has taught me a great deal. Perhaps you don't know our landlord here in the house, but you should; he is a strange man."

"No, I don't know him."

"No, of course not—I see that—but you should."

Oh, I thought, yes, maybe. I didn't know this remarkable landlord he was talking about; he might well be something out of the ordinary, but I lived in another house. I kept my thoughts to myself, however.

"I wonder," the old chap answered me. "He has many houses—nearly all of them. He owns yours, too, I think."

"Yes," he went on, "he's a great one for managing and arranging everything. When I came and asked if he could perhaps house me here, as I, too, had to live somewhere, he eyed me narrowly for a long time.

"'Well, I shall have to put you in the basement,' he said. 'You can't live up in the house itself.'

"'No,' I answered, 'I see that.'

"'I think the basement will suit you,' he said. 'I hope I'm not mistaken about you? What's your own opinion?'

"'I think it would do nicely for me there.'

"'Yes. You know, don't you, that I won't have just anyone there. No bitterness and hatred, no wicked or undependable people. Upstairs I have to take in all kinds, many whom I know very little about, but in the basement I want good, reliable people, people I know and like. What do you think—do you belong here?'

"'I'd like very much to think so,' I answered happily.

"'Well and good. But can you pay the rent?' he said, for he's strict, too—that he is. 'Everyone must pay; there's no getting out of it, however wretched you are. You can have it cheaply, as you're not fit for much. But you must pay something at all events. How will you scrape it together?'

"'I shall have to live on the good people in the world.'

"'Are there any?' he asked, looking at me sharply.

"'There must be many, surely.'

"'That is right,' he said. 'That is easy to work out for anyone who really wants to. You are a man of sense ; you shall live with me.'

"Yes, he is remarkable, though so simple and natural. He has helped me over much. I couldn't get on without him. Every now and then he looks in and sits for a while, talking. It's such a help. It cheers one up being appreciated. 'You're a worth-while man, Lindgren,' he says. It does one good to hear that."

He looked at me in glad content. "Are you a worth-while man?" he asked.

I made no answer, but looked down at the floor, not wanting to meet his eyes.

"One should be," he said. "It helps one over a lot to know that one is."

The room about us was plain but snug. The lamplight shone over the low table with its sawn-off legs, over the cloth where his saved-up bread lay, over the bed on which he took his rest. He paid no attention to my silence. He was sitting with his own thoughts, I could see.

Then he got down from the chair, saw to the fire, washed up the cups and put them on the shelf where they belonged; crept to the bunk and made it ready, folding up the bedcover. But when he had folded it across the seat of the chair and smoothed it, he remained kneeling there.

"It's good when the day is over," he said. And one could see that he was tired.

"Is it, Lindgren? When life is so full and means so much to you?"

"Yes," he answered, looking quietly in front of him, "life is full. I know that so well, I feel it so surely and firmly inside me. But each day is heavy to bear.

"I tell you this because I think we understand one another so well. And one mustn't pretend to be better than one is."

He drew a deep breath. Seeing him huddled together there on his knees, one might have thought he was praying, but he was just made like that.

I got up quietly to go, went up and thanked him, said good-night. He thought I should come back when I felt like it, and I said I should like to. Then he crept with me to the door and I was standing out in the street again.

The whole house was in darkness now. Even the first floor where the chandeliers had blazed just now. It could not have been a real party if it was already over. The old man's lamp was the only one burning; it lighted me nearly all the way home.

The Evil Angel

AN evil angel passed along the deserted streets in the middle of the night. The storm howled between the rows of houses, raged up above in the darkness; there was not a soul to be seen, only he. He walked hunched against the wind, coarse and sinewy, tight-lipped. About his body was a blood-red mantle which concealed the huge wings. He had broken out of the cathedral; he had stood there long enough in the musty stench. Century after century he had smelled the reek of wax candles and incense under the vaults; century after century he had heard songs of praise and the mumble of prayers to a god who hung dead above his head. For centuries he had seen people kneeling with their eyes raised, gabbling everything they believed in. This craven mob, stinking of faith in a pack of lies! This sickening jumble of bewilderment, worry and pitiful hope of being let off, of still being able to clutch on! Now he had broken out!

He had risen out of his fetters and trampled on the altar with his sinewy foot, knocking over the holy vessels. He had stepped down in wrath on to the floor of the church and kicked aside the hassocks. The saints hung round about with their pious, ecstatic faces; the relics inside the gratings smelt decayed; in a side chapel, where a light was burning, a child lay on musty straw and a mother of wax knelt beside it—all this litter of lies and stupidity! Kicking open the doors, he stood outside in the windy night.

Only he was true!

He walked into the streets, stood and looked about him. Oh, so this was how they lived—humankind.

He stopped in front of the doorway of a house, looking

up at it with burning eyes. Then he scratched a cross on the door with the sword he was carrying. "You shall die!" he said.

Then he went to the next, crouching; the wings attached to the enormous shoulders gave him the appearance of being hunchbacked. There, too, he stopped, scratched the cross again. "You shall die," he said.

So he moved from one house to the next, scratching with the sword, which was short and thick, as if for slaughtering.

"You shall die. You shall die. And *you* shall die. And *you* shall die.

"And *you*!"

He went on through the whole town, battling against the wind, forgetting no one.

When he had finished he went outside the ramparts, out into the night where no one lived. There he threw off his mantle and stood naked. And spreading out his wings he flew away into the wide open darkness.

When people awoke in the morning they were all surprised to find a cross drawn on their houses. But they were not frightened. They wondered how it had happened and why it had been done; talked about it before going as usual to their work. Why had this well-known sign been carved everywhere? There was so much else of greater importance of which to remind them.

They knew quite well that they were going to die, they said.

The Princess and All the Kingdom

ONCE upon a time there was a prince, who went out to fight in order to win the princess whose beauty was greater than all others' and whom he loved above everything. He dared his life, he battled his way step by step through the country, ravaging it; nothing could stop him. He bled from his wounds but merely cast himself from one fight to the next, the most valiant nobleman to be seen and with a shield as pure as his own young features. At last he stood outside the city where the princess lived in her royal castle. It could not hold out against him and had to beg for mercy. The gates were thrown open; he rode in as conqueror.

When the princess saw how proud and handsome he was and thought of how he had dared his life for her sake, she could not withstand his power but gave him her hand. He knelt and covered it with ardent kisses. "Look, my bride, now I have won you!" he exclaimed, radiant with happiness. "Look, everything I have fought for, now I have won it!"

And he commanded that their wedding should take place this same day. The whole city decked itself out for the festival and the wedding was celebrated with rejoicing, pomp and splendour.

When in the evening he went to enter the princess's bedchamber, he was met outside by the aged chancellor, a venerable man. Bowing his snow-white head, he tendered the keys of the kingdom and the crown of gold and precious stones to the young conqueror.

"Lord, here are the keys of the kingdom which open the

74

treasuries where everything that now belongs to you is kept."

The prince frowned.

"What is that you say, old man? I do not want your keys. I have not fought for sordid gain. I have fought merely to win her whom I love, to win that which for me is the only costly thing on earth."

The old man replied, "This, too, you have won, lord. And you cannot set it aside. Now you must administer and look after it."

"Do you not understand what I say? Do you not understand that one can fight, can conquer, without asking any reward other than one's happiness—not fame and gold, not land and power on earth? Well, then, I have conquered but ask for nothing, only to live happily with what, for me, is the only thing of value in life."

"Yes, lord, you have conquered. You have fought your way forward as the bravest of the brave, you have shrunk from nothing, the land lies ravaged where you have passed by. You have won your happiness. But, lord, others have been robbed of theirs. You have conquered, and therefore everything now belongs to you. It is a big land, fertile and impoverished, mighty and laid waste, full of riches and need, full of joy and sorrow, and all is now yours. For he who has won the princess and happiness, to him also belongs this land where she was born; he shall govern and cherish it."

The prince stood there glowering and fingering the hilt of his sword uneasily.

"I am the prince of happiness, nothing else!" he burst out. "Don't want to be anything else. If you get in my way, then I have my trusty sword."

But the old man put out his hand soothingly and the young man's arm sank. He looked at him searchingly, with a wise man's calm.

"Lord, you are no longer a prince," he said gently. "You are a king."

And lifting the crown with his aged hands, he put it on the other's head.

When the young ruler felt it on his brow he stood silent and moved, more erect than before. And gravely, with his head crowned for power on earth, he went in to his beloved to share her bed.

Paradise

AND the Lord said: "Now I have arranged things for you here as best I can; planted rice, peas and potatoes, many edible plants which you will find useful, various kinds of grain for baking bread, cocoanut palms, sugar cane and turnips; marked out ground suitable for pasture land and gardening; provided animals that are easy to tame and wild animals for hunting; laid out plains, valleys and mountainous regions, terraces that can well be used for growing grapes and olives; set out pines, eucalyptus trees and fair acacia groves; devised birch woods, lotus flowers and breadfruit trees, violet slopes and wild strawberry patches; invented the sunshine—which you'll find will please you; put the moon in the heavens so that you'll have something to go by till you're big enough to get a clock; hung up the stars to guide you on the sea and lead your thoughts—those that are not of the earth; seen that there are clouds to give rain and shade, thought out the seasons and determined their pleasant changing, and one thing and another. I hope you will like it.

"But remember to eat of the tree of knowledge, so that you will be really sensible and wise."

And the first human beings bowed deeply and humbled themselves before their Lord. "Thank you very much," they said.

They began to dig and cultivate the soil, to reap, multiply themselves and fill the whole of paradise, and they liked it very much. They ate freely of the tree of knowledge, as the Lord had told them, but did not grow noticeably sensible. They became very sly and artful and intelligent, and well-informed and excellent in many

77

ways, but they did not become sensible. And this made their existence increasingly complicated and troublesome, and they got into more and more of a muddle.

At last a resolute man appeared who was grieved by the way things were going, and he stepped forward before the Lord and said: "The people are behaving so strangely down there, it seems to me; it's true they grow more intelligent and shrewd every day, but they prefer to turn their cunning and great learning to evil and senseless uses; I don't know, but there must be something wrong with the tree of knowledge."

"What," said the Lord, "something wrong with the tree of knowledge, did you say? Certainly not. It must be like that, don't you see? It's the best I could do. If you think you know what it ought to be like, then please say."

No, he didn't know. But all was not as it should be down there, and however well-thought-out the tree of knowledge might be, it did seem as though eating from it made them a little foolish.

"But the tree cannot be otherwise," the Lord said. "Admittedly, it's rather complicated learning how to eat of it, but it must be complicated; it can't be helped. Some things you must find out for yourselves, or what's the point of your existence? You can't be spoon-fed the whole time. Personally, I think the tree is the finest thing I've created, and if you don't show yourselves worthy of it, human life won't be much to speak of. Tell them that."

And with that answer the man had to be content.

But when he had gone the Lord sat there quite distressed. If they had found fault with anything else he had made, it wouldn't have mattered so much, but the tree of knowledge was especially dear to his heart, perhaps because it had been so much more difficult to make than the other trees and everything else on the earth. Like the great artist he was, he was thinking at this moment not of his generally recognized achievements but only of this misunderstood work into which he thought he had secretly put his whole soul, without having any joy of it. And just because this very work of his seemed to him so extremely important, he couldn't imagine that humanity could do without it— its real, deep significance.

And perhaps he was right. He was, after all, a great creative spirit and ought to know best himself. He ought to know what he had put his soul into.

He sat thinking that people were ungrateful to him and his most outstanding work.

It is not easy to know how long he sat thus. Perhaps time passes quickly in eternity and the wingbeats of the Lord's thought are perhaps as thousands of years for us. Then a man came again before him, but this time it was the archangel Gabriel himself who came.

"You have no idea what it's like down in paradise," he said. "It is quite incredible. They are trying to destroy everything for you and they think of the worst imaginable deeds of villainy to bring it about. There is a deafening noise and they hurl the hideous fruits of the tree of knowledge at each other so that they burst with a horrible roar, and, worst of all, uproot all the vegetation. They bluster and brag so that it's shameful to hear them and they say they're much cleverer than God himself, for they invent much greater things than you, and they have frightful monsters that shatter everything in their path, everything that you have created, and in the air they have huge imitation birds that vomit fire and devastation. I have never been in hell—I'm glad to say—but that's what it must look like. It is an abomination. And it's all the fault of that tree of knowledge. You should never have given it to them—and come to that, I said so from the outset. Think what you like, but have a look at how things are there!"

And the Lord looked down on to the earth and saw that it was true. Then wrath was kindled in his mighty, pained creator's soul and lightning flashed from his eyes and he sent out his hosts and they drove the people out, together with all their evil and devilish works, into the great desert of Savi, where nothing grows. And he set a fence around paradise, and two angels at its gate, each with his machine gun and flaming sword. And the desert lay right next to paradise and the fence round about.

Inside, life was delightful with its sun and verdure, fresh and springlike now that the people had been driven out; the meadows smelled sweet and the air was full of bird song. And the banished stood looking in between the bars and saw it, but they could not get in.

And the angels—those who were not on guard—retired to rest after the battle and fell asleep, exhausted. But under the best-loved tree in paradise the Lord sat in deep contemplation, and its branches shaded him with their great peace.

The Children's Campaign

EVEN the children at that time received military training, were assembled in army units and exercised just as though on active service, had their own headquarters and annual manœuvres when everything was conducted as in a real state of war. The grown-ups had nothing directly to do with this training; the children actually exercised themselves and all command was entrusted to them. The only use made of adult experience was to arrange officers' training courses for specially suitable boys, who were chosen with the greatest care and who were then put in charge of the military education of their comrades in the ranks.

These schools were of high standing and there was hardly a boy throughout the land who did not dream of going to them. But the entrance tests were particularly hard; not only a perfect physique was required but also a highly developed intelligence and character. The age of admission was six to seven years and the small cadets then received an excellent training, both purely military and in all other respects, chiefly the further moulding of character. It was also greatly to one's credit in after life to have passed through one of these schools. It was really on the splendid foundation laid here that the quality, organization and efficiency of the child army rested.

Thereafter, as already mentioned, the grown-ups in no way interfered but everything was entrusted to the children themselves. No adult might meddle in the command, in organizational details or matters of promotion. Everything was managed and supervised by the children; all decisions, even the most vital, being reached by their own little general staff. No one over fourteen was allowed. The boys then passed automatically into the first age-group of the regular troops with no mean military training already behind them.

The large child army, which was the object of the whole nation's love and admiration, amounted to three army corps of four divisions: infantry, light field artillery, medical and service corps. All physically fit boys were enrolled in it and a large number of girls belonged to it as nurses, all volunteers.

Now it so happened that a smaller, quite insignificant nation behaved in a high-handed and unseemly way toward its powerful neighbour, and the insult was all the greater since this nation was by no means an equal. Indignation was great and general and, since people's feelings were running high, it was necessary to rebuke the malapert and at the same time take the chance to sub- jugate the country in question. In this situation the child army came forward and through its high command asked to be charged with the crushing and subduing of the foe. The news of this caused a sensation and a wave of fervour throughout the country. The proposal was given serious consideration in supreme quarters and as a result the commission was given, with some hesitation, to the chil- dren. It was in fact a task well suited to this army, and the people's obvious wishes in the matter had also to be met, if possible.

The Foreign Office therefore sent the defiant country an unacceptable ultimatum and, pending the reply, the child army was mobilized within twenty-four hours. The reply was found to be unsatisfactory and war was declared immediately.

Unparalleled enthusiasm marked the departure for the front. The intrepid little youngsters had green sprigs in the barrels of their rifles and were pelted with flowers. As is so often the case, the campaign was begun in the spring, and this time the general opinion was that there was something symbolic in it. In the capital the little commander-in-chief and chief of general staff, in the presence of huge crowds, made a passionate speech to the troops in which he expressed the gravity of the hour and his conviction of their unswerving valour and willingness to offer their lives for their country.

The speech, made in a strong voice, aroused the greatest ecstasy. The boy—who had a brilliant career behind him and had reached his exalted position at the age of only twelve and a half—was acclaimed with wild rejoicing and from this moment was the avowed hero of the entire nation. There was not a dry eye, and those of the many mothers especially shone with pride and happiness. For them it was the greatest day in their lives. The troops marched past below fluttering banners, each regiment with its music corps at the head. It was an unforgettable spectacle.

There were also many touching incidents, evincing a proud patriotism, as when a little four-year-old, who had been lifted up on his mother's arm so that he could see, howled with despair and shouted, "I want to go, too. I want to go, too!" while his mother tried to hush him, explaining that he was too small. "Small am I, eh?" he exclaimed, punching her face so that her nose bled. The evening papers were full of such episodes showing the mood of the people and of the troops who were so sure of victory. The big march past was broadcast and the C.-in-C.'s speech, which had been recorded, was broadcast every evening during the days that followed, at 7.15 p.m.

Military operations had already begun, however, and reports of victory began to come in at once from the front. The children had quickly taken the offensive and on one sector of the front had inflicted a heavy defeat on the enemy, seven hundred dead and wounded and over twelve hundred prisoners, while their own losses amounted to only a hundred or so fallen. The victory was celebrated at home with indescribable rejoicing and with thanksgiving services in the churches. The newspapers were filled with accounts of individual instances of valour and pictures several columns wide of the high command, of which the leading personalities, later so well-known, began to appear now for the first time. In their joy, mothers and aunts sent so much chocolate and other sweets to the army that headquarters had to issue a strict order that all such parcels were, for the time being at any rate, forbidden, since they had made whole regiments unfit for battle and these in their turn had nearly been surrounded by the enemy.

For the child army was already far inside enemy territory and still managed to keep the initiative. The advance sector did retreat slightly in order to establish contact with its wings, but only improved its positions by so doing. A stalemate ensued in the theatre of war for some time after this.

During July, however, troops were concentrated for a big attack along the whole line and huge reserves—the child army's, in comparison with those of its opponent, were almost inexhaustible—were mustered to the front. The new offensive, which lasted for several weeks, resulted, too, in an almost decisive victory for the whole army, even though casualties were high. The children defeated the enemy all along the line, but did not manage to pursue him and thereby exploit their success to the full, because he was greatly favoured by the fact that his legs were so much longer, an advantage of which he made good use. By dint of forced marches, however, the children finally succeeded in cutting the enemy's right flank to pieces. They were now in the very heart of the country and their outposts were only a few days' march from the capital.

It was a pitched battle on a big scale and the newspapers had enormous headlines every day which depicted the dramatic course of events. At set hours the radio broadcast the gunfire and a résumé of the position. The war correspondents described in rapturous words and vivid colours the state of affairs at the front—the children's incredible feats, their indomitable courage and self-sacrifice, the whole morale of the army. It was no exaggeration. The youngsters showed the greatest bravery; they really behaved like heroes. One only had to see their discipline and contempt of death during an attack, as though they had been grown-up men at least.

It was an unforgettable sight to see them storm ahead under murderous machine-gun fire and the small medical orderlies dart nimbly forward and pick them up as they fell. Or the wounded and dying who were moved behind the front, those who had had a leg shot away or their bellies ripped open by a bayonet so that their entrails hung out— but without one sound of complaint crossing their small lips. The hand-to-hand fighting had been very fierce and a great number of children fell in this, while they were superior in the actual firing. Losses were estimated at 4000 on the enemy side and 7000 among the children, according to the secret reports. The victory had been hard won but all the more complete.

This battle became very famous and was also of far greater importance than any previously. It was now clear beyond all doubt that the children were incomparably superior in tactics, discipline and individual courage. At the same time, however, it was admitted by experts that the enemy's head-long retreat was very skilfully carried out, that his strength was evidently in defence and that he should not be underrated too much. Toward the end, also, he had unexpectedly made a stubborn resistance which had prevented any further penetration.

This observation was not without truth. In actual fact the enemy was anything but a warlike nation, and indeed his forces found it very difficult to hold their own. Nevertheless, they improved with practice during the fighting and became more efficient as time went on. This meant that they caused the children a good deal of trouble in each succeeding battle. They also had certain advantages on their side. As their opponents were so small, for instance, it was possible after a little practice to spit several of them on the bayonet at once, and often a kick was enough to fell them to the ground.

But against this, the children were so much more numerous and also braver. They were everywhere. They swarmed over one and in between one's legs and the unwarlike people were nearly demented by all these small monsters who fought like fiends. Little fiends was also what they were generally called—not without reason—and this name was even adopted in the children's homeland, but there it was a mark of honour and a pet name. The enemy troops had all their work cut out merely defending themselves. At last, however, they were able to check the others' advance and even venture on one or two counter-attacks. Everything then came to a standstill for a while and there was a breathing-space.

The children were now in possession of a large part of the country. But this was not always so easy. The population did not particularly like them and proved not to be very fond of children. It was alleged that snipers fired on the boys from houses and that they were ambushed when they moved in small detachments. Children had even been found impaled on stakes or with their eyes gouged out, so it was said. And in many cases these stories were no doubt true. The population had quite lost their heads, were obviously goaded into a frenzy, and as they were of little use as a warlike nation and their cruelty could therefore find no natural outlet, they tried to revenge themselves by atrocities. They felt overrun by all the foreign children as by troublesome vermin and, being at their wits' end, they simply killed whenever they had the chance. In order to put an end to these outrages the children burned one village after the other and shot hundreds of people daily, but this did not improve matters. The despicable deeds of these craven guerrillas caused them endless trouble.

At home, the accounts of all this naturally aroused the most bitter resentment. People's blood boiled to think that their small soldiers were treated in this way by those who had nothing to do with the war, by barbarous civilians who had no notion of established and judicial forms. Even greater indignation was caused, however, by an incident that occurred inside the occupied area some time after the big summer battle just mentioned.

A lieutenant who was out walking in the countryside came to a stream where a large, fat woman knelt washing clothes. He asked her the way to a village close by. The woman, who probably suspected him of evil intent, retorted, "What are you doing here? You ought to be at home with your mother." Whereupon the lieutenant drew his sabre to kill her, but the woman grabbed hold of him and, putting him over her knee, thwacked him black and blue with her washboard so that he was unable to sit down for several days afterward. He was so taken aback that he did nothing, armed though he was to the teeth. Luckily no one saw the incident, but there were orders that all outrages on the part of the population were to be reported to headquarters. The lieutenant therefore duly reported what had happened to him. True, it gave him little satisfaction, but as he had to obey orders he had no choice. And so it all came out.

The incident aroused a storm of rage, particularly among those at home. The infamous deed was a humiliation for the country, an insult which nothing could wipe out. It implied a deliberate violation by this militarily ignorant people of the simplest rules of warfare. Everywhere, in the press, in propaganda speeches, in ordinary conversation, the deepest contempt and disgust for the deed was expressed. The lieutenant who had so flagrantly shamed the army had his officer's epaulettes ripped off in front of the assembled troops and was declared unworthy to serve any longer in the field. He was instantly sent home to his parents, who belonged to one of the most noted families but who now had to retire into obscurity in a remote part of the country.

The woman, on the other hand, became a heroic figure among her people and the object of their rapturous admiration. During the whole of the war she and her deed were a rallying national symbol which people looked up to and which spurred them on to further effort. She subsequently became a favourite motif in the profuse literature about their desperate struggle for freedom; a vastly popular figure, brought to life again and again as time passed, now in a rugged, everyday way which appealed to the man in the street, now in heroic female form on a grandiose scale, to become gradually more and more legendary, wreathed in saga and myth. In some versions she was shot by the enemy; in others she lived to a ripe old age, loved and revered by her people.

This incident, more than anything else, helped to increase the bad feelings between the two countries and to make them wage the war with ever greater ruthlessness. In the late summer, before the autumn rains began, both armies, ignorant of each other's plans, simultaneously launched a violent offensive, which devastated both sides. On large sectors of the front the troops completely annihilated each other so that there was not a single survivor left. Any peaceful inhabitants thereabouts who were still alive and ventured out of their cellars thought that the war was over, because all were slain.

But soon new detachments came up and began fighting again. Great confusion arose in other quarters from the fact that in the heat of attack men ran past each other and had to turn around in order to go on fighting; and that some parts of the line rushed ahead while others came behind, so that the troops were both in front of and behind where they should have been and time and again attacked each other in the rear. The battle raged in this way with extreme violence and shots were fired from all directions at once.

When at last the fighting ceased and stock was taken of the situation, it appeared that no one had won. On both sides there was an equal number of fallen, 12,924, and after all attacks and retreats the position of the armies was exactly the same as at the start of the battle. It was agreed that both should claim the victory. Thereafter the rain set in and the armies went to earth in trenches and put up barbed-wire entanglements.

The children were the first to finish their trenches, since they had had more to do with that kind of thing, and settled down in them as best they could. They soon felt at home. Filthy and lousy, they lived there in the darkness as though they had never done anything else. With the adaptability of children they quickly got into the way of it. The enemy found this more difficult; he felt miserable and home-sick for the life above ground to which he was accustomed. Not so the children. When one saw them in their small grey uniforms, which were caked thick with mud, and their small gas masks, one could easily think they had been born to this existence. They crept in and out of the holes down into the earth and scampered about the passages like mice. When their burrows were attacked they were instantly up on the parapet and snapped back in blind fury. As the months passed, this hopeless, harrowing life put endurance to an increasingly severe test. But they never lost courage or the will to fight.

For the enemy the strain was often too much; the glaring pointlessness of it all made many completely apathetic. But the little ones did not react like this. Children are really more fitted for war and take more pleasure in it, while grown-ups tire of it after a while and think it is boring. The

boys continued to find the whole thing exciting and they
wanted to go on living as they were now. They also had a
more natural herd instinct; their unity and camaraderie
helped them a great deal, made it easier to hold out.

But, of course, even they suffered great hardship.
Especially when winter set in with its incessant rain, a cold
sleet which made everything sodden and filled the trenches
with mud. It was enough to unman anyone. But it would
never have entered their heads to complain. However bad
things were, nothing could have made them admit it. At
home everyone was very proud of them. All the cinemas
showed parades behind the front and the little C.-in-C. and
his generals pinning medals for bravery on their soldiers'
breasts. People thought of them a great deal out there, of
their little fiends, realizing that they must be having a hard
time.

At Christmas, in particular, thoughts went out to them,
to the lighted Christmas trees and all the sparkling childish
eyes out in the trenches; in every home people sat wondering how they were faring. But the children did not think
of home. They were soldiers out and out, absorbed by their
duty and their new life. They attacked in several places on
the morning of Christmas Eve, inflicting fairly big losses on
the enemy in killed and wounded, and did not stop until it
was time to open their parcels. They had the real fighting
spirit which might have been a lesson even to adults.

There was nothing sentimental about them. The war
had hardened and developed them, made them men. It
did happen that one poor little chap burst into tears when
the Christmas tree was lighted, but he was made the laugh-
ing-stock of them all. "Are you homesick for your mummy,
you bastard?" they said, and kept on jeering at him all
evening. He was the object of their scorn all through
Christmas; he behaved suspiciously and tried to keep to
himself. Once he walked a hundred yards away from the
post and, because he might well have been thinking of

flight, he was seized and court-martialled. He could give no reason for having absented himself, and since he had obviously intended to desert he was shot.

If those at home had been fully aware of the morale out there, they need not have worried. As it was, they wondered if the children could really hold their ground and half-regretted having entrusted them with the campaign, now that it was dragging on so long because of this nerve-racking stationary warfare. After the New Year help was even offered in secret, but it was rejected with proud indignation.

The morale of the enemy, on the other hand, was not so high. They did intend to fight to the last man, but the certainty of a complete victory was not so general as it should have been. They could not help thinking, either, how hopeless their fight really was; that in the long run they could not hold their own against these people who were armed to the very milk teeth, and this often dampened their courage.

Hardly had nature begun to come to life and seethe with the newly awakened forces of spring before the children started with incredible intensity to prepare for the decisive battle. Heavy mechanized artillery was brought up and placed in strong positions; huge troop movements went on night and day; all available fighting forces were concentrated in the very front lines. After murderous gunfire which lasted for six days, an attack was launched with great force and extreme skill. Individual bravery was, if possible, more dazzling than ever. The whole army was also a year older, and that means much at that age. But their opponents, too, were determined to do their utmost. They had assembled all their reserves, and their spirits, now that the rain had stopped and the weather was fine, were full of hope.

It was a terrible battle. The hospital trains immediately started going back from both sides packed with wounded and dying. Machine guns, tanks and gas played fearful havoc. For several days the outcome was impossible to foresee, since both armies appeared equally strong and the tide of battle constantly changed. The position gradually cleared, however. The enemy had expected the main attack in the centre, but the child army turned out to be weakest there. Use was made of this, especially because they themselves were best prepared at this very point, and this part of the children's front was soon made to waver and was forced farther and farther back by repeated attack. Advantage was also taken of an ideal evening breeze from just the right quarter to gas the children in thousands. Encouraged by their victory, the troops pursued the offensive with all their might and with equal success.

The child army's retreat, however, turned out to be a stratagem, brilliantly conceived and carried out. Its centre gave way more and more and the enemy, giving all his attention to this, forgot that at the same time he himself was wavering on both wings. In this way he ran his head into a noose. When the children considered that they had retreated far enough they halted, while the troops on the outermost wings, already far ahead, advanced swiftly until they met behind the enemy's back. The latter's entire army was thereby surrounded and in the grip of an iron hand. All the children's army had to do now was to draw the noose tighter. At last the gallant defenders had to surrender and let themselves be taken prisoner, which in fact they already were. It was the most disastrous defeat in history; not a single one escaped other than by death.

This victory became much more famous than any of the others and was eagerly studied at all military academies on account of its brilliantly executed, doubly effective encircling movement. The great general Sludelsnorp borrowed its tactics outright seventy years later at his victory over the Slivokvarks in the year 2048.

The war could not go on any longer now, because there was nothing left to fight, and the children marched to the capital with the imprisoned army between them to dictate the peace terms. These were handed over by the little commander-in-chief in the hall of mirrors in the stately old palace at a historic scene which was to be immortalized time and again in art and even now was reproduced everywhere in the weekly press. The film cameras whirred, the flashlights hissed and the radio broadcast the great moment to the world. The commander-in-chief, with austere and haughty mien and one foot slightly in front of the other, delivered the historic document with his right hand. The first and most important condition was the complete cession of the country, besides which the expenses of its capture were to be borne by the enemy, who thus had to pay the cost of the war on both sides, the last clause on account of the fact that he had been the challenging party and, according to his own admission, the cause of the war. The document was signed in dead silence, the only sound was the scratching of the fountain pen, which, according to the commentator's whisper, was solid gold and undoubtedly a future museum piece.

With this, everything was settled and the children's army returned to its own country, where it was received with indescribable rapture. Everywhere along the roads the troops were greeted with wild rejoicing; their homecoming was one long victory parade. The march into the capital and the dismissal there of the troops, which took place before vast crowds, were especially impressive. People waved and shouted in the streets as they passed, were beside themselves with enthusiasm, bands played, eyes were filled with tears of joy. Some of the loudest cheering was for the small invalids at the rear of the procession, blind and with limbs amputated, who had sacrificed themselves for their country. Many of them had already got small artificial arms and legs so that they looked just the same as before. The victory salute thundered, bayonets flashed in the sun. It was an unforgettable spectacle.

A strange, new leaf was written in the great book of history which would be read with admiration in time to come. The nation had seen many illustrious deeds performed, but never anything as proud as this. What these children had done in their devotion and fervent patriotism could never be forgotten.

Nor was it. Each spring, on the day of victory, school children marched out with flags in their hands to the cemeteries with all the small graves where the heroes rested under their small white crosses. The mounds were strewn with flowers and passionate speeches were made, reminding everyone of the glorious past, their imperishable honour and youthful, heroic spirit of self-sacrifice. The flags floated in the sun and the voices rang out clear as they sang their rousing songs, radiant childish eyes looking ahead to new deeds of glory.

God's Little Travelling Salesman

T HE train clattered along on the little branch line, knocking the buffers and jolting the sweaty passengers. It was the height of summer, the sun blazed down, beating in through the rattling windows and making the thin metal walls hot to the touch.

"Yes, ungodliness is rampant in the world, you can hardly sell a thing," a little man of about forty said to himself as he sat squeezed in among the others in a third-class carriage. "It is grievous to see. People don't need God's word nowadays. And they're stingy too. When it comes to anything like that they haven't a penny to spare. It's just the same in town. Business is as bad there, of course. But it doesn't matter, as long as Jesus is with us. It is good to have *him*. To know that you are in *his* service. It's glorious to have been chosen for something like that. . . . Awful the heat here. All the windows are shut because of the draught. Yes, that must be why."

He leaned against the smoky windowpane and looked out. The sparse, monotonous countryside crawled past, swamps with one or two stunted firs in the tussocks, slopes with juniper and bilberry, now and again a wood which lasted for a while, and then swamps again. Here and there was a cottage with a patch of tilled ground, but there was never anyone to be seen. It was a poor part of the country. Silly to come here really. But they needed God's word so badly. Though it was even worse elsewhere. When folk become prosperous they have little use for Jesus. It was glorious to spread the word among those who hungered for it, to go forward as a sower over this stony ground. It was a great and blessed mission. Of a truth he was chosen for it.

In the town there were supposed to be a lot of saved and as a rule they were fairly well off. Things ought to go better there. But they were probably stingy too. They usually were. And they had their mission bookshop there of course. But as long as Jesus is with us it's all right. As long as he blesses our work. Yes, it's good to be able to lay our sorrows on him. It's not always so easy to be his instrument in this world.

He looked at the people in the compartment to see if there were any who appeared to be saved. It was hard to say. They stared straight in front of them the whole time and didn't speak. Their faces were lean, ugly, void of thought. When the train lurched they bumped against each other and then sat motionless again. They seemed rather tired and sweated in the heat. Opposite him were a farm hand and a middle-aged peasant woman, asleep. The farm hand was healthy and coarse and had a flushed face; his legs were stuck straight out under the other seat and he breathed heavily in his sleep. The woman was huddled in the corner, thin and wizened, there was no sound of her breathing and no sign either; the toothless mouth was open, gaping like a hole, as if she were dead. It was hard to say what was their relationship to God, whether they had received their Saviour's grace.

Yes, they probably had bad preachers in this out-of-the-way part of the world. He had heard one on Sunday who was not up to much. It depended a lot on the servant God chose. Yes, the man had had no delivery at all, just stood talking in a meek voice, and he himself couldn't help thinking that if *he*, Emmanuel Olsson . . .

But what was the use. . . . It was long ago. No, he was not cut out for a preacher.

But at least he had had the gift for it! No doubt of that. He could seize people's souls, carry them with him. When the spirit came upon him, he spoke so that they were moved. He was moved himself by his words, so no wonder they were, too. People came from all over the place. Of course they thought he was not worth hearing. He was not wanted anywhere. That's the way of the world.

But it didn't matter. He had served his God anyway. He had done his best. We all have our failings, we're only human.

Anyway, it was just as well he had stopped that preaching. For his own salvation it was best. All that speaking had filled him with the sin of pride, which is the worst of all.

It cut him to the heart to see these poor people here in the third class, sitting so dumb, so poor and barren in spirit. He would like to have preached to them, spoken to them of their Saviour, given them solace in their silent need. But it was not his business. He was not fitted for it. Still, he did what little he could through his work, tried to spread God's message, his words of comfort among these poor unfortunates who toiled and eked out an existence here in the backwoods. Even so, perhaps a few seeds fell on good ground.

The train stopped at a station and some men entered the compartment. They were rather noisy. "Nice and warm for you bastards in here, isn't it?" one of them said as he came in. They were a little drunk, it seemed. One had a bottle in an inside pocket and they went on drinking as soon as they sat down. When the conductor came the men put the bottle under the seat. They talked at the top of their voices and the whole compartment woke up, came to life; everyone sat listening to the stupid things they said and all the faces were grinning broadly. A girl had to look out of the window because of the things they said. The peasant woman woke up, turned around in a daze and looked at them sternly, her mouth awry and sleepy. Then, putting on her kerchief, she settled down in the corner and smiled at their ridiculous behaviour. The farm labourer sat up with a start, wide awake at once like a child, shoved his arm over the back of the seat and gave a grin. And the men felt encouraged, it seemed; they grew even more talkative and facetious than before, drank and bandied words.

It was strange that they dared to drink, it was forbidden. But he didn't judge them. Oh no. It was sad, very sad, but he judged no one. He himself had his faults; no one is perfect. He didn't make himself out to be holy as other believers did. He was humble, as a Christian should be. He was tolerant and quiet. Sat looking at their goings on without abhorrence and wrath in his gaze. It was the pure stuff they were drinking, he noticed. They were going to finish the bottle, by the look of it. But he didn't judge. It was not his business.

The train stuttered along in the summer heat; the engine wheezed on the upgrade so that the smoke trailed past the windows. And the men bawled and sang. Words were no longer enough in which to express themselves. Suddenly the carriage lurched going around a bend and the passengers were thrown together in a heap. The bottle slid from the hand of the man who was holding it and smashed on the floor. A stream of oaths gushed over the carriage strong enough to shiver it. They kicked the broken bits of glass under the seat, swearing volubly. Then they burst out laughing because that had bitched their drink, as they said, and became friends again.

The heat was insufferable, the liquor stank on the floor, the men sprawled with their arms around each other's necks, bawling and shouting. But he sat there without judging, meek and quiet.

These people were wandering in the dark, indeed they were. But then they hadn't any preachers who could proclaim the word properly for them. And they spent their money like this, and when they went to buy a sorely needed tract they had nothing, they couldn't afford it of course. The saved couldn't afford it either, come to that. It's all the same whether people have money or not when it's a matter of that. Well, he'd see how things went in the town; it was better than wearing himself to a thread on the roads anyway. He ought to be able to sell something anyway.

They must be there now. The wheels clattered, they were already in the station yard. It was certainly not small; there were cars loaded with timber and grain everywhere on the tracks, wood lay stacked up along the line, with the company signs and telephone numbers. It's a busy place, I can tell you. It might be all right, there were people at any rate. Yes, here we are!

He stepped down on to the platform, small and agile. Quite down at heel, he looked, though the others around him were only simple people, too. His clothes were greasy and his shoes were split, but he had a frock coat. Under his arm he carried a grubby paper parcel tied up with twine. He set off into the town to try to do business.

It was bigger than he had thought. And it seemed prosperous, too. Might be all right. He might just as well start straight away.

Not far down the street he passed a small haberdasher's shop. He might try there. It wasn't so bad as a rule; he had sold several booklets in a haberdasher's once. They were usually peaceable folk who kept such shops. He went in.

There was no one there, but after a moment a woman came out of a door that was ajar. There was something very quiet and melancholy about her, so he had come to the right place all right.

"Can I interest you in a small tract today?" he asked.

"No thank you," she answered in a distressed voice.

But he undid his parcel and spread out what he had on the counter, as you must do; you mustn't give in straight away. Showed the different things and recommended them.

"No, thank you," she said.

"This one is particularly good *The Way to Jesus*, very popular."

"No, thank you."

"Perhaps this one then, *Chosen Thoughts on a Christian's True Conduct*, also a great favourite. . . ."

"No, thank you."

"Oh, not today then."

"No."

"Well, good afternoon."

Well, he would have to try somewhere else. It always took a while. Best to go into the apartment houses, of course. He went in at the next doorway, rang a bell on the first floor; downstairs there was nobody at home. An elderly woman with a very refined, pleasant appearance opened the door.

"Can I interest you in any religious tracts today? Good books which are very popular. . . ."

"No, thank you," she said with an infinitely gentle smile.

"Perhaps this excellent book, cloth-bound, *Sin and Grace*. . . ."

"No, thank you very much."

"Nothing at all today?"

"No, thank you."

"Well, I'm sorry to have troubled you."

"Oh, not at all."

"Good afternoon, thank you."

Yes, of course. He might have known it. He would have to try next door.

A corpulent woman opened the door, perhaps the wife of the shopkeeper on the ground floor.

"Can I interest . . ."

"No, thank you."

"*The Spring of Life* . . ."

"No, we don't want any."

"Here's an excellent little booklet, *The Way to Jesus*, much in demand, only these two left."

"No, we don't want any."

"The lady next door bought it."

"Oh? Who?"

"I don't know. She was elderly. Rather thin."

"Oh?"

"Yes, a very refined lady."

"Oh, I know! Mrs. Berglöv! Oh, did *she* buy it? . . ."

"Yes, she had heard so much about it, but it is so hard to come by."

"Oh—Oh, I'd better take that one then."

"Thank you very much, ma'am. Good afternoon."

Another family lived across the landing.

"Can I int . . ."

"No, you can't," a woman snapped.

"The lady opposite bought this little book. . . ."

"It's no business of mine what that old crone buys," she snorted, and banged the door.

It was terrible the way he always struck women. And they were the worst. Meanest at any rate.

He'd have to try the next. No, they didn't want anything. And the next. No, they didn't want anything. And the next. No—o.

This street then? No, they didn't want anything.

Well, what did he say! He knew it. What was he to do? And the sun blazed down. You couldn't sell the word of God in weather like this, of course. Sweating on the stairs, up and down and up and down.

What was he to live on? He must get something toward food, and a roof. . . .

He crossed the street, better luck there perhaps? Went in at random. Must be a kind of office, he saw, after he had rung the bell. A man hurried out in his shirtsleeves.

"What do you want?"

"Can I interest you in God's . . ."

"Good heavens, no!" the man said, slamming the door.

This was hopeless. He couldn't go on aimlessly like this. He would have to find out the right ones. After all, there were supposed to be quite a lot of saved here.

He asked a mild-looking man if he could tell him where
the mission hall was? Yes, it was in such and such a street,
just keep right on, he couldn't miss it. . . . The voice was
so calm and subdued that he ventured to ask if he would
care for a few religious pamphlets. No, he wouldn't. So
that was wrong, too, of course.

He would go along and find out how the land lay. It was
a long street, and went uphill. At last the stone pavement
came to an end and there at the top was the mission hall;
yes, that must be it, a brown-painted building on an open,
neglected piece of ground. There were no curtains at the
windows so you could see it wasn't an ordinary house but
served a special purpose. He went around and looked;
there was a smaller door at the back and a window with
curtains. That must be where the caretaker lived. He
knocked at the door.

A woman of about sixty came out with a dust cloth in
her hand. He told her why he had come. Had heard that
there were so many saved here in the town, wondered
where they all were, how he could sell a few tracts. . . .

"Oh, I can't help you. . . ."

No, but perhaps she could give him the names of some
who usually liked such God-fearing literature and who
could well afford to buy?

"Oh no, I don't dare; you see they might get angry with
me for having sent you."

Yes, he understood that, but he wouldn't say it was she
who sent him.

Hm. . . . She looked at him rather distrustfully and
thought it over. Did he need to sell then?

"Yes," he said tonelessly, "indeed I do."

She asked him into the kitchen, which was also her
room. "Yes, it'd be awful if they found out I had sent you,
I tell you!" Oh, not for the world!

"Are things really so bad?" she said, after asking him
to sit down. She was a kind soul, he could see that. He told

her how badly things were going. People don't need God nowadays.

"No, that's true, that's true," she said, rocking her head.

Perhaps she'd like a tract herself?

"Lord save us, I don't need that, living here. I hear so much of God's word, there's nothing else in this place. And I've no head for reading; it makes me feel queer after a while. I leave that to others, and to them as can afford it. There's not much to live on here, I can tell you."

"No, I suppose not."

"You look poorly," she said, looking at him more closely. "Would you like a drop of coffee? It's all made." He would indeed; he was touched and surprised at such kindness.

"Oh, it's only Christian," she said.

"But look at me with the dust cloth in my hand! I was cleaning up in there. . . . Sit up to the table now," she said, pouring out the coffee.

She sat down herself to rest her legs, they got so stiff. "The cleaning there is in this place, real fed up I get sometimes. They mess the place up every time, of course, such a lot of people come. You see, we've got a preacher who preaches ever so well; it's wonderful to hear God's word like that, but it means a lot of work. We haven't had a revival to touch it all the thirteen years I've been doing the cleaning here—I haven't lived here more than eight, see, but I've cleaned for thirteen. There was a man called Andersson before that, he was a carpenter really, but sickly. Yes, what a preacher! Then they wanted a woman; he was no use, just moved a few chairs about at the meetings."

He sat without speaking. "Have another cup, do," she said, looking at him pityingly, at his clothes and the like.

"No, it's not so easy, I can tell you. And then my old man died, but I'd done such a lot of scrubbing for readers —superior readers, of course—so I got this place. Yes, God be praised. Thank you, Jesus. He arranges everything for the best for us all. But it hasn't always been so easy, with three youngsters to feed until they could fend for themselves. Now I don't have to do so much, and a good thing, too. I'm not up to it; wore out I am with that blessed floor in there, it takes such a time. But I don't complain. And after all it's something to clean in God's house. It's not like going out cleaning."

He asked if by any chance she knew anyone who might buy a few things. . . .

"Oh yes, I was quite forgetting! Let me see now. . . ." She thought of several people in the town who would no doubt be glad to buy. He wrote down their names and where they lived and thanked her profusely for doing him such a great favour.

And Mrs. Berglöv—she nearly forgot—he must go to her—she was sure to buy something.

"Is she saved?" he asked.

"Yes, I should just think so; she's one of the best that comes here to the meetings. Very refined lady, and very godly."

"Oh, she said nothing about that."

"Have you been to her?"

"Yes."

"And she didn't buy anything! Well, I never. . . ."

Well, she must get the floor finished. There was to be a big revivalist meeting this evening and it must have time to dry, but it soon would in this heat.

He asked if he could go in with her and look at the hall. Goodness yes, of course he could. They went in together.

It was the same as always. He stood on a dry patch in the middle of the hall and looked at the bare walls, panelled and painted a grey-brown colour; behind the platform hung a garland because it was summer. Although it was scrubbed so often he could smell that special smell which was always the same. He felt something heavy in his breast. The woman had started her scrubbing again. He went cautiously toward the platform, stepping where it was driest. Mounted the pulpit, stood looking out over the hall. The woman was busy scrubbing and did not look up —he made a slight gesture with one hand.

Then he went back with his head bowed. Well, he'd be going now. She came and held out her wet hand, and saw that he had tears in his eyes.

"What's wrong?" she asked.

He didn't answer, just turned away.

"No, it's not so easy," she said, "it's not so easy. . . ."

They said good-bye.

He walked down the hill. Well, he'd begin again then. One address was in a side street a little way down. He tried there first. No, they didn't want anything, not today. Farther along on the same side there was another. But not there either. They had so many godly tracts, a whole shelf as he could see. Then he made his way to a family in another street. He got no for an answer there, too. Odd, he had heard that they were believers.

"And who told you that, may I ask?"

"The woman who looks after the mission hall; she said that this was such a very religious family."

"Oh, did she. . . . Well, we'll buy a small tract then."

He got rid of *In Jesus' Footsteps*, one of the cheapest. The next he came to was a tailor. He was squatting on the table, gaunt and shrunken, and looked wanly at him from behind his glasses.

"I don't buy from that quarter," he said after glancing at the books.

"Don't you? I heard that . . ."

"Yes, that's true enough. But I belong to the Baptists," he explained in a quiet voice.

"O—oh, I see."

"Yes, so I read *our* tracts."

"Yes, I quite see. But there are all kinds here, edifying

stories from life, like this moving little account, *A Soul in Need*."

"Thank you, but you see I only read *ours*."

It was no better at the next house. He tried by saying that the woman at the mission hall had sent him. "Oh, she talks so much, that woman," they said. He had to agree with them, but they didn't want anything, all the same. He went on, asking his way until he found the people he was looking for. "I sell this book a lot; it seems to be very popular here." That was nice to hear. But they were not needing anything. Thank you, not today.

He grew apathetic and tired of it all, but kept on all the same, up and down stairs, from one house to another. At one place he sold a small booklet to a kind and helpful person, but otherwise nothing.

Evening was drawing on. He came to a family who were in a great hurry. They were putting on their coats in the hall and had no time for him at all. "I suppose you've got the hymnbook, Elvira dear," the mother said with a sigh. "Well, let's go then."

Of course, they were going up to the mission hall. They turned the key in his face as he stood with his hat in his hand and one or two tracts held out like a hand of cards when the game is nearly over. He followed them out into the street, still with his hat in his hand like a beggar. "There you are," said a fat man on his way into a restaurant, holding out a copper coin. He thanked him confusedly.

Then he just drifted along the pavement. People hurried past. Far away in a park a band was playing; now he heard it, now he didn't. A man came out of an eating-house and lurched away, hugging the wall.

"No, I'm not going to stand about gaping any longer!" he said to himself, and went in through the door which the man had left half open behind him.

Inside, the air was smoky and smelt of beer and food.

"Bring me something to eat, please, something cheap," he said when he had found a seat. The place was crowded, there was a buzz of noisy voices. Nice to rest for a while, sit down at least—anywhere. There were aquavit glasses laid on every table. So spirits were served here. Supposing he were to have one too. He could do with it after such a day. Perhaps it was terribly dear at a place like this. He'd better ask. No, it wasn't. That was a good thing, when he was so poor.

The waitress brought the food and the other. He tossed the aquavit off at once; it was best beforehand. Then he ate for a while and it tasted good. It all did him good, stimulated. He felt a different man.

"No, it's not my fault," he said to himself. "I have fought against it. That I have. But when you have such disappointments and worries, no one can hold out."

No, God tried him too hard. Even that can go too far. He had hoped so much to sell something in this town, came here with such burning hopes. Like an envoy of the Lord he had trudged around, knocking on doors, on people's hearts. But what had happened? How had he been received? How much had he sold?

No, his disappointments and worries were too great. It was too much to bear. It really was. Not so strange if he took another dram. That was only right, surely.

The waitress came and filled up the glass. He could feel it doing him good.

It was quite a good place, this. It really was. For the price. Nice and homely atmosphere, talk and laughter. He could certainly do with it after toiling from morning till late at night—trying to work, trying to offer people what their souls needed, spiritual food. . . .

Yes, it may look as though I'm a bad man, but I'm not. I'm filled with the spirit in *my* way.

I can only be filled with the spirit in my own way.

No, I'll say it again. It's not my fault. I'm only an

ordinary, imperfect human being and have never made myself out to be anything else. A bad servant. . . . Yes! I won't deny it. I'm imperfect, I say it myself. I *am*. But why have you chosen me then, if I don't suit? I ask you that, my Lord and God. *Why have you?*

Here I sit among sinners—drinking—in a low dram shop. . . . It's bitter, it's *bitter*. . . .

He became sunk in his sorrows; much of his former life passed before his eyes.

Think what I could have had—if I'd gone on with the career I had chosen. . . . I had a good job, I'd soon have been head salesman. Might even have had my own little shop by now. And I'd have been upright in my dealings. And I'd have been a believer. Gone along to the mission hall every Sunday to hear God's word. . . .

Yes, if I'd only stayed with Lindström's. . . . But you had given me gifts, I was to witness for you, spread your message in the world. It wasn't enough that I was saved. I was to devote my whole life to you. For you had *called* me! So I took my small savings in order to study at the mission school. . . . I was to preach your word as none other. I thought you intended me for something great. . . .

But I found out that you didn't. You had others who were much better. . . . And I was sent now here, now there. . . . Yes, I realized I had misunderstood you. Things only got worse as time went on. . . .

And then they said that he drank! He didn't! Perhaps just a drop once or twice because he felt so depressed and thought that God couldn't be bothered with him. But he didn't *drink*.

And anyway it's not so strange if you have a drop now and again when God forsakes you. When he leaves you alone on the road, although you have sacrificed all in order to follow him, *all*. . . .

"Give me another one, you there. . . ."

And when I was done for as a preacher—how was it

now? Yes, I remember! It was so *unjust*! The greatest
injustice ever committed against anyone! When I stood
there in the pulpit. . . .

No, I can't. . . . It's too bitter. . . .

I was speaking God's pure words, wasn't I! I was filled
with the spirit as never before! I felt so inspired, it was
glorious, glorious. . . . I remember quite well. . . .

And they—they thought I was drunk!

It's a lie! I hadn't touched a drop that day. I may have
taken a little now and then—I don't deny it—I don't make
myself out better than I am. But not that day! I only spoke
more feelingly because I was so moved—it was the most
beautiful moment in my life. I was so moved that I had
tears in my eyes. . . .

And they thought it sounded muddled. . . . When I
spoke so clearly, with such fire. . . .

And supposing he *had* wanted to make himself con-
spicuous, because they thought he was nothing—was it so
strange? He needed work, yes of course he did. But he
wasn't thinking of that when he spoke—he was so filled
with the spirit, with God's grace. . . . Perhaps he wasn't
filled with it? Perhaps what he had felt had been wrong?
But how could he be so moved deep inside, so clearly sense
God's presence, if it was only to get the vacant position
there?

Yes, it's worried me ever since that day. How is it
possible?

No, I don't understand. I'm only asking, that's all.

It had finished him. After that he had never pulled up.
Then he had become as he was—had to take to the roads—
try to sell a few tracts—eke out an existence—in poverty,
poverty. . . .

He put his head in his arms, sat there and cried. Yes, cry,
go on. . . . I can well understand why you cry. . . . The
way you've suffered—scorned, rejected by all—like a tramp
—on the roads—sleeping in barns—getting a bite of food

here and and a bite there—And trying again—again—again—with your bundle under your arm—trying to spread your Lord's message. . . .

"No, my God, haven't you tried me too hard? Yes, I tell you, you're too *hard*. . . . Why have you chosen me for your high calling—and then forgotten you've done so. . . . And I've gone on all the same, with what I thought was right—alone, forsaken, lost—with your calling inside me, which wasn't withdrawn either, for that matter—with what you put in my heart after all, and which doesn't go out so easily once it's been lit, no, not so easily. . . . Going around selling tracts—destitute and wretched for your sake—until I sit here boozing. . . ."

He raised the glass, which had been refilled. His hand shook slightly because he was so moved.

"If it be possible, let this cup pass from me," he mumbled with tears in his eyes. "Nevertheless, not my will, but thine, be done. . . ."

Awful how tipsy this made him. It was because he could never afford a decent meal, of course. . . .

Yes, it was the spirit which had prompted him! He only said what *it* said! So much for that! Lured into something he wasn't fitted for! And then just down and down, into shame and degradation. . . . I was an upright man before I got into all this. . . . Yes, it was the spirit! It had made him blab—puffed him up, made him more than he was, so that his fall would be all the greater. . . . That was it! He had been chosen—and then he was done for—he had been tricked in some way—and here he sat—drunk—a poor wretch—when he could have had his own little business. . . .

He had been tricked, that's all there was to it!

The publican came and put his coarse hand on his shoulder.

"You can't sit here getting drunk!" he said. "We're closing now. Out with you."

"Drunk! I'm not drunk! It's a lie!"

"Get out now!"

"It's a sheer lie! Just because a man is so moved—gets tears in his eyes—and then they say he's drunk! It's . . ."

He was given a shove through the door, he reeled across the pavement and landed up in the gutter.

Perhaps he had struck his head. Or perhaps he just lay there, unable to get up.

A Salvation Army sister passed by on her way from a meeting. When she saw him she was horrified, took a step back. Then she went forward and helped him up. It was difficult, his legs would not support him and she was not strong enough. He could hear a thin, faint sound all the time, it sounded so funny. It came from a string of the guitar which she had over her shoulder in an oilcloth cover. At last she got him to his feet. "My poor man," she said, holding on to him because he was swaying. "What do you think Jesus would say if he saw you like this?"

"Whassat?" he snuffled.

"Give up your sinful life. Come to the Army one evening. All are welcome, even those who have fallen lowest. Come to Jesus."

"Oh, go to hell!" he said, wrenching himself free.

He lurched about the streets, came to a small park, lay down under a bush and fell asleep.

When he woke up in the morning he no longer had his bundle with the religious tracts. He had lost it. He went and asked at the eating-house but was shown the door; they knew nothing about any bundle. He must have dropped it. It was gone anyway. Oh well, it didn't matter.

He had no money, either. He went from door to door begging. Here and there he got a few coppers, enough for bread. At nights he slept in a timber yard somewhere.

He did not really feel any more wretched than before

with this life. It was freer in some way and seemed easier to him, whatever the reason. But he had a hard time of it. There was never enough to satisfy his hunger, and he got nothing to drink. He had to watch out for the police, too, because he went around begging. He wasn't used to that. And the vagabonds who stood behind the woodpiles swigging their beer would have nothing to do with him and never gave him a drop. He was not one of them, either, because he had a kind of frock coat.

No, he had never had such a bad time. You can get used to anything, but still . . . He became the most wretched-looking of all the vagabonds in the town. He grew starved and gaunt and at last had no strength left. He was ill, too, or so he felt. It was all up with him.

Then one evening he saw a Salvation Army officer in the street. And he remembered what the Salvation sister had said. . . . Supposing he were to go along? He followed the officer, perhaps he was on his way to the Army.

And so it was. He went inside.

There was singing and playing. He sat huddled on a bench right at the back and listened. It was good to sit down. And no one turned him out. It felt so peaceful and safe here. Now the testimonies began, they spoke of Jesus, of their Saviour. Testified to his grace, to how he had called them to him. All the well-known words. O dear Jesus, thanks be to thee. He clasped his hands. His lips moved as he repeated the words in a whisper. His eyes shone as he looked up at the light. It was as if he had come home again.

Up on the platform stood the officer who had helped him that evening. Putting down her guitar, she came and prayed with one or two on the benches while the captain went on playing softly. She knelt with one after the other, whispering in a voice of implicit faith. At last she came right down to where he was sitting. She recognized him at once. "Is it you, my friend? Oh, I knew that you would come!" she said, and her face shone with joy. "Kneel with me before Jesus our Saviour and pray that he may have mercy on your soul."

They knelt and prayed together, fervently, long, more and more ecstatically. He confessed his sins, what a lost sheep he was. He cried as a child.

When at last he got up he was another man; his eyes shone with a secret bliss. He had been saved once more!

Reverently he left the hall, went and lay down in the timber yard. Lay there awake in quiet happiness with an old sack he had found under his head. Saw the summer stars kindle in the heavens, so pale that they were hardly visible.

After that he went to every meeting. They took care of him, gave him clothes and food. They were good people, didn't judge as others did. They received you just as you were. You had a soul just the same which was of value to God.

In time they helped him to become an officer, when they discovered his gifts and who he really was. He had passed his examination, though such was not accepted here at the Army, and he had his experience as a preacher. In due course he became a lieutenant. After some years he was even made captain for the corps here. Things went well for him, his time of suffering was past.

All were very pleased with him, and they had reason to be. He had become so completely changed. He never drank again, he had dedicated himself utterly to God. When he testified, he spoke very beautifully but always quietly, never overdid it, though here at the Army they didn't mind a little fervour. But everything he said was full of heartfelt, burning faith. In his testimony he often touched on how he had lain in the gutter when he had suddenly been called by his Saviour through the medium of an officer who was passing. "Come to Jesus!" she had said, and he had followed. He was even ready to speak of this after he had reached a sufficiently high position to gloss over his early days had he wanted to. But that was how low *he* had once fallen. He made himself out no better than he was, he never had.

They thought he was a purified soul. And he was too, in his way; he *had* been purified. They knew that he had been through a lot. And that he had been a great sinner. But Jesus had worked miracles with him.

He realized that himself. And he never ceased to thank God for having led him in his mysterious way to this town where, after sufferings endured, he was again to proclaim God's word, find his right vocation. How strange it was that just when he stood on the brink of ruin, when he could so easily have forsaken the Lord's path and left his true calling, Jesus had chosen that moment to take him back and give him the service for which he was best fitted. He had devoted all his life to God. That was his mission. That was why he was received back into the service of the spirit. That was where he belonged and where he was needed.

And something was attained by him through this. He really did become a better man, even if not entirely a different one. No one does. He was at least honest now. Perhaps curbed, more humble in spirit, but in any case genuine, what there was. When he was careful not to exaggerate in any way, he *became* honest and sincere, he had noticed. And now that he was no longer so harassed by the fact that he wanted them to like him—to accept him, by his anxiety to get work, all that he said and felt was in itself so much more genuine. That is how it is. Life had put him—as all of us—in its school and moulded and fostered him, purged his inner being, made him of greater worth.

Nor was he ever as bad as may perhaps appear from this account of him. He had his faults, that is true. But who has not? There was no harm in him really, nothing special. With him, as with so many others, it was just that he had a slovenly soul.

The Masquerade of Souls

This story takes the reader to the land where the souls are. We know that everything there is perfect, is beautiful and sublime, not like here. Beings whom we cannot quite comprehend, whom we can only vaguely imagine, live their glorified life there. They have their existence above the world of reality and humiliation. Only perfection may prevail with them, wherever one goes, wherever one's dazzled eye looks. Such is the soul's land, where it has its real home. And in that land there is always festival. There it is always masquerade.

IT was a fashionable party at an exclusive restaurant, supper with dancing. Two young people had chanced to sit together at one of the small tables. They did not know each other beforehand. But for some reason they were soon captivated by each other in a strange way. It was not a hasty infatuation the first time they met; it was something deeper, harder to explain—a strong, inner feeling which brought them face to face, both just as questioning and almost helpless. They knew that their very beings were drawn together, though they had never met before, knew nothing about each other. It was something they had never experienced, a mystery to them.

They sat looking at one another with strangely blank faces. Spoke abstractedly—what was it they had said? What had they just been talking about? Everything seemed so unimportant, even this. They seemed to be so bared to each other because of what was going on inside them that words could only obscure. There was really nothing to be said. Nothing they wanted said. They just talked all the same. Fell silent and talked again. But their minds were hushed by a kind of reverence.

He looked at this face, so perfectly beautiful that he thought he had never seen anything even superficially resembling it. The dark eyes with their soft and shyly appealing expression; a look that was strangely fascinating without wanting to be, which was solitary in some way and appeared ever on the alert, like a bird ready to fly deeper into the forest at the slightest rustle in the trees, at a leaf which did not fall silently to the ground. And with this the purest features, delicate, formed by the gentlest hand, but perfect in their almost spiritual fragility; a complexion of a curious, warm paleness which was broken by the fine line of the brow; the hair drawn tightly back, glossy black, enhancing the fineness of the brow and the pure, almost inevitable beauty of the whole head.

Because the face was so fragile, the mouth perhaps seemed redder and fuller than it was. In some way it had its own particular life and expression, was half open and hot as after a kiss. The arms, too, in their soft repose had this sensual quality, and so did the figure, slender but softly feminine in the tight-fitting white silk dress. It was a beauty which might well have been challenging, proud and radiantly self-centred. Perhaps part of the fascination lay in the fact that she was not at all like that, in this contrast between the outer and the inner, between her splendour and this warm, inquiring look, at once submissive and alert, shy but also free, occasionally left quite alone in the deep eyes.

He did not understand this contrast which so attracted him. He merely felt her nature such as it was. He merely sensed her. With a strange clarity he felt her proximity, that she existed here beside him. And a great, secret happiness because of it.

Was it possible that this woman could also be interested in him? He divined it, must believe it, though it seemed far too conceited. He had a certain power over women, mostly when he bothered least about it. But this was something so utterly different. It was not a case of that—not with this being. If she felt attracted to him it must be because she sensed instinctively a deeper affinity with something in him. He didn't know what. But he felt unworthy. Unworthy as never before in the presence of anyone he had met.

He was quite a handsome young man, perhaps a little older than she. He looked the usual man about town, but only his exterior; one soon noticed something distinctive about the lean, tall figure with the face that was so often very grave. There was a certain smouldering intensity about him, about this dark face, about his whole behaviour. Something of uneasiness, almost of fanatical excitement. It was apparent sometimes even in his manner—a slight nervous agitation, a certain impulsiveness in his gestures, even when he only adjusted his tie or stroked back his hair, something feverish. But not so much now, not at this moment of strange stillness in her presence, of watching and somehow listening for something. His inner self merely gave an animated expression to the characteristic, already distinctive features, something gentle, almost fragile to the young manliness of the face.

They were so taken up with each other without actually wanting to show it that at last they had to smile. A little reluctant smile which came over them both simultaneously. It was a relief. It brought them together more than if something had been said, something which could not have been said as it should. They smiled at one and the same thing —in complete understanding. They had something in common, an undefined secret which was not to be revealed, which *couldn't* be, for in one way it was nothing. Could be *thought* nothing. Like the sparkle in a cobweb, something which can turn grey and paltry at the slightest touch. But it was delightful, wonderful just as it was. And it was more real than anything else, than the people and the hum around them, than their own words—trite, ordinary words which they exchanged; than the whole grey net over the world. The two, so recently strangers to each other, already shared something great, impalpable, unforgettable. They had this smile, a silent familiarity with something strange, unknown. It felt like an adventure, exciting, uncertain. And were they not in fact smiling with happiness at having met?

What were they speaking of now? It was surely about something else, about what was really important to them, what they were interested in, about what they thought, their views on this and that. But now and then they would break off and smile. They were only words, after all, something one says.

But they might just as well speak of it. Like two people standing side by side—two on a journey, perhaps far away in a foreign country—talking rapturously about what they are seeing together, about the scenery, the view, delighted that everything is so fascinating and beautiful—until one of them puts his hand on the other. What are you thinking of?

But suddenly they just talked about themselves. All at once it seemed quite natural to pass on to that, to start talking about their lives, their inner selves. They suddenly found they could speak without reserve. Spoke eagerly, excitedly—until they smiled at their eagerness. A strange smile, which glided away, glided into earnestness. They fell silent, both at once, glided into silence—like two people standing beside each other at the railing in the twilight. The shore fades away and the sea and sky—there is not even the sound of the wind in the sails, in the rigging—on a soundless voyage into the unknown, the two of us. Who are you?

He noticed that for some reason there was something poignant in her smile. Something sad. Not exactly when she smiled, but just as the smile vanished. A tiny, almost imperceptible line by the mouth, in this infinitely sensitive skin which was so close to him that he could make out every nuance; the fine down lent a delicate, untouched bloom to her face, as with a child. Only a hint of pain, but something surged up in him when he saw it, a violent feeling of—he didn't know what. Of tenderness, goodness; he wanted to sacrifice, understand, wanted to live for something, make something great and glorious of his life, make one big sacrifice of it. And then this look which drew him to it without seeming to want to, which revealed itself in all its shy warmth—did he not follow it right in to where it was alone, into her soul, her world?

Strange—two people meeting. What is more vague, intangible and yet suddenly capable of giving such a secret infinitude to life and such a revelation of it? Merely because you sense another's being, someone who is alive, who exists, who is quite close to you.

You yourself exist. But that is nothing. Only you. But the fact that this being really exists fills you with wonder. It is as though life had disclosed itself to you, its essence, its very mystery.

Around them was the hum of the big restaurant. Music was playing, dancing had begun, long ago probably. They noticed nothing, seemed unaware of it. He did ask her once if she wanted to dance, for it occurred to them where they were—and to float away with her seemed to him suddenly the most wonderful of all and so absolutely in keeping with their mood. But she merely shook her head in answer.

No, she was right. What was going on inside them was far too rare. They couldn't go and jostle with people, not now. Must be alone with each other.

And they really were, in the midst of this crowd and noise. All these people, the gay, brightly lighted room, meant nothing to them as they sat there in each other's presence, held by something which was so remote from this world. They seemed no longer part of it. Another world had opened for them, more wonderful than anything in their dreams. They were lifted up into its sphere, into the world where they knew that they must live from now on, only there. Were lifted by an unspoken, jubilant happiness which they knew they shared.

The whole evening passed without their being aware of time. They just existed, those two, existed for each other, confiding their innermost being, their thoughts—their whole soul. When at last it was time for everyone to go, they felt they had known each other a whole lifetime and been joined by invisible bands.

He asked with a smile if they, too, ought not to be making a move. Yes, she nodded. They felt almost sad at having to tear themselves away from this moment in which they had met, from the whole place, from the table in its cosy corner where they had experienced this unforgettable evening. But they were not going to part! No, no. There was no question of their separating. Not any more.

He gave her a long, tender look of thanks, and they got up. Walked toward the door, she in front and he a few steps behind her.

He stopped for a moment, as though his attention had been drawn to something. She was lame.

The vestibule was crowded. He seemed very eager, as though they were in a hurry. "Where is your wrap? Is it here, or over there? May I help you—if you'll just give me your number. Thank you! I'll get your things. Sit here for a moment, I won't be long."

He elbowed his way in among the others, who made way reluctantly. Got jammed in. Stood there waiting. Turned over the number checks; one was 5, the other 127. 5 and 127. He had to wait a long time. When at last he got up to the counter he stood watching the others get their coats; forgot to hand over the checks. A rough push finally roused him. He was given his coat and a soft, silk-lined beaver wrap. It had a lovely warm feeling, as such fur coats have. He squeezed his way out of the crush.

"Here you are, at last! It takes ages."

He helped her on with it. And with her rubber boots. When she was sitting it was not noticeable. The right calf was perhaps a shade thinner than the other.

They walked downstairs in silence. She evidently found the stairs difficult. So it seemed to him at least. She held on to the rail.

Outside was a clear winter sky, stars. The slush had frozen but it did not feel cold.

"It's nice and fine now," he said, putting his hands in his pockets.

"Yes," she answered with a slight tremble. "You'd never have thought so this morning. Awful weather we've had, dark and grey. Good thing if it's real winter soon. All this greyness makes you so depressed."

"Yes—but I'm forgetting! Wouldn't you like a taxi?" No, she preferred to walk. It was odd. But she did. Thought it was nice to get out in the air for a while.

"All the better. May I see you home?"

"Yes, if you like. There is nothing I'd like better."

They walked along the street. "I should think it's started to freeze," he said.

"Yes, I should think so."

"What's the time, by the way? A quarter past one! As late as that. Time *has* gone quickly."

"Yes, you don't notice it when you sit talking like that," she said.

"It was quite a nice party, don't you think, as far as those things go?"

"Yes—"

"Nicely arranged. And the reception rooms are quite grand now that they've been done over. Rather banal, of

course, but still . . . not so bad really. Don't you think so?"
"Yes."

They fell silent. He could hear from her walk that she was limping.

They stopped at a cross street. They turned up here, didn't they? He chanced to meet her eyes in the lamplight. They confused him in some way. Had they a new expression? Mocking? No, it was nothing like that. It was only dead earnest, just as before, but even deeper. And quite open, however far in he wanted to look. It was so open that it appeared indifferent; it merely regarded someone. But her expression had something burning within, its own strangely shimmering fire.

They went on up the side street. There was no one about; their footsteps were the only sound.

"It's been a wonderful evening," he began ardently in another voice, the one he had had when they were sitting inside.

"Do you think so?" she said tonelessly, as though indifferent.

"Yes, I do. It's so seldom one can talk like that to anyone."

"Oh, don't you usually?"

"What chance is there? It must be something so very rare. Unfortunately—I must confess it's never happened to me before. And you?" he asked.

"Yes, I think it was a nice evening."

He glanced at her; at a car which ran past with the little rear light; and at the shut-up shops, iron shutters nearly all the way along. Seemed to be nothing but shops. . . .

"It was rather odd," he went on. . . . "I mean, just by chance like that . . ."

"What?"

"That we happened to meet."

"Yes, it was."

He buttoned a glove which had come undone. Adjusted the scarf inside his coat collar.

"It meant a lot to me," he said. "Being able to sit and talk like that. It's so stimulating. Don't you think so too? And with a woman. It's rather unusual. I don't think it's ever happened to me, I must say."

"No, I suppose it's not usual," she said flatly and seemed tired.

They turned into another street where there were more people. And then again into a more empty one. It looked deserted, badly lighted. Was rather a dreary quarter.

"What do you usually talk to women about, then?" she asked at last, when nothing had been said for a long time.

"Oh," he laughed, "about anything at all. The same as everyone talks about on such occasions, I suppose. But it bores me, to be quite honest.

"No," she said hesitantly. "For my part I must say that I don't much care to talk to a man in that way. It doesn't suit me."

"No, that's what I felt."

"Did you?"

"Yes, and that's what I value so highly. I'm no good at this superficial game that's always played the minute a man and woman happen to meet."

"Oh, why not?" she said. "There's no harm in it."

"No—of course not. . . ."

"There's no need to take it too seriously either."

They did not speak for a while. Crossed the street to turn the corner.

"Then we could have sat talking in quite another way this evening," he threw out.

"Yes, perhaps."

"And you would have preferred that?"

"No—o I wouldn't. I didn't say that. . . ." Her voice was a little unsteady.

"It's hard for me to imagine how else we could have entertained each other," he said.

"Yes. . . . It felt so natural for us to talk as we did."

"That's what I think. . . ."

He was silent for a while.

"Usually one is careful not to say anything one means," he went on. "That's the form of conversation one is most used to. But—I don't know. It would never have occurred to me to talk like that to *you*."

"I'm so glad you say that!" she answered, turning her face toward him. He could not see it properly, but he heard from her voice that it must have lighted up.

They walked more slowly—for it couldn't be so much farther—and walking could not have been easy for her, not as easy as it appeared; it was not possible. And she shouldn't exert herself. There was no hurry.

They began talking. More than before they touched on much they had discussed then—more casually perhaps; they could speak of it better now, in fact without restraint. They could go into things more, explain their thoughts more clearly to each other. And yet feel the joy of the intimacy between them.

"You know," he said at last, "I feel as if we had so much in common. Don't you think so, too?"

"Yes. I do."

"That must have been why we were drawn together like that so quickly. In such a friendly way. It's not really easy for either of us to confide in another by the look of things. It's not for you, is it? No, nor for me. But it felt quite natural. . . ."

"Yes. . . ."

"For my part I feel as if I had found a friend. And before I was quite alone."

She looked at him swiftly, as if in quiet, shy happiness.

"That's how I feel too," she said softly.

"Yes—" he began after a moment, breaking their silence, "how alone one is among people, when you think of it. It's like being among strangers."

"It's like that with me too."

"That must be what I noticed about you. . . . I expect you're also the kind that prefers to keep to yourself."

"I suppose I've got used to it."

"But now we've found a really good friend—both of us. Haven't we?"

"Yes," she answered gaily.

They were filled with solemnity, a tranquil joy at what they felt within them. They had walked past the house where she lived and had to turn back. Stood outside the door.

He took her hand. He could feel its warmth through the glove, as if it were bare. They were facing each other once more; he saw her again for the first time since their first meeting, her pure beauty with this reserved gravity which gave such a deeply personal character. Her eyes were shining when they met his. Then they seemed to change, take on a softer glow, more warmth. And the face had that strange bareness, that light and animation from within. . . .

Suddenly he put his arms round her and kissed her violently, her lovely, half-open mouth which grew large and soft as she wrenched herself free. "No, no," she gasped, escaping inside the door. He followed, but she held him at arm's length imploringly. They stood there panting, unable to speak. Just whispered softly of when and where they were to meet. Then she pushed him away and vanished inside.

He strode back along the street, his heart pounding. He could hear himself breathing. . . .

What was it? For a moment he seemed almost to have forgotten; everything stood still. He felt something moist on his mouth and pulled out his hand to wipe it away—no —he put it in his pocket again; saw her in front of him, her face, cheek—her temple—her ear hiding in her hair. And something soft which glided away from his lips. . . .

Yes. . . . But just how had it happened?

He ought not to have . . .

No, it was foolish of him, surely it was.

Why? Well, of course . . .

It was *wrong*. . . . He had acted *wrongly*. . . .

But how delightful she was—and what a wonderful person! *Must* be. . . . With that reserve, that shyness that concealed so much—something strong—alive—what a strange creature she was. . . .

The thought of her flowed through him, of her soul such as he divined it, sensed it within himself like a new, secret life he had received as a gift, fragile—something serene, burning. . . .

Think—to give oneself up to such a being, utterly, entirely—with all one's thought and dreams. . . . For *always*, for *life*. . . .

Hm—isn't it strange? When at last we meet—when we meet another, a kindred soul, one to whom we feel drawn. . . .

It's strange all right. . . .

He turned up his collar and plunged his hands deep into his pockets. The wind felt cold as he turned into the promenade.

But why was he rushing like this? He would soon be home, he could take it more quietly. After all, it was pleasant to walk for a while, late at night like this. . . .

Yes. . . . It was just that he had kissed her. Nothing else. . . . No, it had been a wonderful evening—un-forgettable. . . .

Yes—*unforgettable*. . . .

As he walked along he looked up at the winter sky gleaming above the branches of the trees, huge and solemn; became rapt in thought. . . . He stood for a moment outside the door, looked up again at the expanse of sky where the stars were sparkling brightly.

"Yes, it's a funny old world," he said. . . . Then he felt for his door key and went upstairs. Undressed, rather absently, got into bed. Tried to read for a while as he usually did, but his mind wandered. He was thinking of her. Put out the light. Couldn't sleep. Lay in the dark, seeing her image in front of him, pure, transfigured, her wonderfully ethereal face. . . . It was as though she were there. As though he felt her soul inside him, another's soul on a soundless, fleeting visit, mysterious and tense as a bird. . . .

He held his hand tightly pressed against his eyes—they were burning as if from tears. . . .

How bitter—how merciless life is, nothing but pain, pain, even when the most glorious of all meets us. . . .

He fell asleep with hot eyes and his hand still over them as if to keep her with him.

When he woke in the morning he was sleepier than usual. It must be late already. And what was it now? Thought there was something, something special. Yes, of course. Of course. . . . *She.*

He lay thinking, recollecting. It was Sunday, so he might as well lie in for a while. But what was the weather like? Aha, splendid! In that case he would rather get up.

He puttered about the flat. Got out a change of clothes, clean shirt and the rest; started shaving. Lathered his face slowly and meticulously with his eyes in the mirror.

Yes—think, a woman like that, if she hadn't been lame. How sorry he felt for her. Such a pretty girl. Pretty *in every way.* It was really an awful pity. . . .

Yes, yes, of course he wanted to meet her. Very much. About three. . . . He was looking forward to it.

He finished shaving, washed off the soap, dabbed his face with a hot, wrung towel and rinsed it with cold water. Nice. Now he felt more like himself. He dried his hands thoroughly, examined them carefully, cleaned his nails.

But it didn't matter, he thought. *He* liked her just the same. Though of course . . . Yes, he liked her very much, he did really. There was something about her—that was what had attracted him from the first—a certain *something*....

He went and stood by the window as he got his mouth wash ready. Looked out. What a day! Remained there singing softly to himself at the sight of the clear air. Then he returned to his thoughts and his interrupted toilet.

Yes—to be sure. But then she realized that herself. . . . Good Lord—of course she did, that was obvious. . . . He flicked the water out of the toothbrush. Now he would hurry and finish dressing. Put on his shirt, clothes, humming to himself as he usually did when he dressed. Chose a tie to match his suit, stood tying it in front of the bedroom mirror.

Supposing he had known from the outset? Yes, it had been a shock all right. . . .

Now he was ready. Threw on his coat and went out.

The sun was shining, trying to thaw the ice on the road, but in the shade the hoarfrost lay untouched and white. Not at all a bad day. Lovely and bracing. One felt reborn coming out into this. The trees were like strange, dualistic beings in black and white. They seemed in a kind of cheerful mourning—it was beautiful anyway. Quite wonderful. He would go for a really long walk, that's what he would do.

He set off out of the town toward the outskirts, parks and woods, where there was seldom anyone about. It was some hours before he turned for home, somewhat tired, walked more slowly on the way back. The outing had blown away the cobwebs. But this was evidently the end of the good weather. Was starting to cloud over again. . . .

Yes. . . .

The sky pressed down over the town. Everything was in a frosty silver light, cool and refined. . . .

It felt different from before. . . . People looked cold and miserable. It was Sunday. You could tell from everyone that it was Sunday.

No, he'd go and have lunch somewhere now. Was high time. And this was merely depressing.

He jumped on to a tram, came into the city centre. Went and had lunch at a restaurant where he was known. Ordered some wine to liven himself up a bit.

Yes, this was a good way of passing the time. He sat looking out of the window at the misty town. Already the sun seemed to think of setting, the air had a faint pink glow in the raw cold. The water flowing past below the window, broad and icy, reflected the clouds burning red. Beautiful. They had a charm all their own, these miniature days—short, fleeting as human life. . . .

He lit a cigarette with his coffee. Sat looking out at the sky through the smoke.

Yes—he was really looking forward to talking to her. He liked her voice so much—it was unusually pleasant. And it had something—hard to say what—There was always something over and above the words to which one listened.

She was a strange person all right. That elusiveness in her being—like the quivering above great heat—when the air shimmers but the actual fire cannot be seen. . . .

Yes. . . . And there was something so wise about all she said, a personal wisdom. They had the same interests, too. That's why it all went so well when they sat talking together. Yes, they had quite a lot in common. Would probably become good friends. He hoped they would, too, sincerely.

He blew out the smoke, watched the rings float up the pane, which grew misty and then cleared again.

And wasn't it odd—before they even knew each other, had merely exchanged a few commonplace words—And yet they had noticed a mental affinity and understood one another. . . .

He had thought it was so strange—something he had never met with before. . . .

Yes, there might well be a kinship between two souls which is sensed in this way and which fills us with solemnity, with a kind of reverence. Perhaps it is our inner self which, without our help, feels the bond with another being—and we ourselves stand looking on, as it were—pushed a little to the side, like an intruder. That was almost how he had felt it. Perhaps with our coarse senses we are too imperfect to be initiated. We have merely a presentiment—a peep into a world which otherwise is hidden from us. . . .

We know so little about the way things are. . . .

Just something like this must be very unusual—unusual that there is someone to meet. . . .

People are something rare. And it is still more rare that they can be meant for each other as they really *are*, that they can tell each other simply and openly that they exist— *they* of all people.

That is probably why there is so much loneliness in the world.

What was the time? Half-past two. He needn't go just yet.

It was very peaceful here. . . . Was he the only one in the whole restaurant? Yes. . . . Quite empty.

Yes. . . . there was certainly something about it, he had never heard a voice like it. . . . It seemed to deepen and ramify the meaning of everything she said—it became so eloquent and living. Was enlarged to something *more*. . . . It was never one string which sounded within her, always the whole instrument. . . .

A strange, rich instrument. . . .

He knocked the ash off his cigarette. Sat staring out of the window.

Then he came to himself more. Drank up his coffee, which he had forgotten; took another cup to have something to do.

Wasn't it time to go now? Yes. . . .

He started off for the rendezvous. Walked up and down on the pavement. The church clocks struck three.

He looked for her.

Would she come from there or from there? No, from the square probably. But not yet, of course.

He felt quite excited. Yes—the way they had parted yesterday—of course. . . .

What did she think about it? Hard to say. . . .

But her lips *were* so tempting. . . . And just then they had parted, a shade, only a shade. Yes, they had been held together by a slight moisture and then they broke away from each other. . . . It was that which . . .

What was the time? Ten past. She ought to be coming.

The mouth felt large, he had not expected that—soft and with a trembling from within her, though she hadn't wanted to. It was like herself, shy and hot at the same time. . . . Though this was not—one could only imagine how it . . .

A quarter past. Why didn't she come then?

Oh well, women are never punctual—but now it was—it was nearly twenty past. . . .

Supposing she didn't come? Yes, of course. She would come all right. He was absolutely certain of it.

He walked up and down a little more quickly. Up and down.

No, now it was almost half past! Supposing something had happened to her? He would not be able to find out. Not be able to ring. . . . No, he just *couldn't*. Would have to remain in doubt—not know the reason. . . .

He was sure that something had happened to her. Otherwise she would have come.

Though it was a ridiculous idea. . . . Well, she could have been run over as she crossed the street because she was. . . . But there was no reason really; she walked just as well as anyone else. . . .

Now it was striking the half hour. Soon twenty-five to. . . .

This was strange. What was the reason? As long as . . .
There she was! Getting out of the taxi over there.
Well, that was a good thing. . . .

"Have you been waiting?"

"Oh, not long."

"Forgive me, I quite forgot to look at the time."

"Oh, that's all right. Glad you came anyway."

"It's hardly walking weather."

"No, you're right. Shall we go in somewhere instead?"

"No—I don't want to. We can walk for a while anyway.
I must get back soon, unfortunately. We have dinner early
on Sunday, the maid has the evening off—if you know
about such things."

Yes, he did. They walked along by the water. Talked of
this and that.

"What have you been doing today?" she asked.

"Nothing much. Yes, I went for a long walk into the
country."

"Oh."

"It was better weather this morning."

"Yes, it's rather raw now."

They stood looking out over the water a moment, as she
had stopped by the quay. The gulls were wheeling in
screaming flocks through the dusk.

Then she pulled her fur around her and they went on.

"You're not cold, are you?" he asked, bending forward
and looking at her.

"Oh no."

She was wearing a different hat, a little tight-fitting one
which suited her admirably. He saw her head in profile
and as if it had been bare.

"Just think," he said, "I had such a strange feeling as I
was waiting. . . . I got the idea that something had happened to you. . . ."

"To me? But—what?"

She looked at him, rather uncertainly. "Because I was late?" She smiled.

"Yes. . . ."

"But that was no reason to . . ."

"None at all. . . . But I don't know, I'm like that sometimes, my imagination runs away with me."

"I expect you have a very vivid imagination—in many ways."

"Perhaps. . . . You don't approve, I gather."

"Oh yes."

He walked for a while in silence.

"It wasn't so strange that I should be worried about you," he went on. "I couldn't help it. And then I thought that if something had happened to you I couldn't find out. . . .'

"But what could have happened?" she said softly.

"Oh. . . . One gets all kinds of ideas. And it needn't have been an accident—anything unpleasant. . . ."

"Would you care?" she asked with a tremble in her voice.

He stopped.

"Yes. I would," he said.

She, too, stopped and looked at him. A faint smile spread over her face, so fleeting and shy that it merely seemed to wonder if it would stay longer. When it vanished, it seemed to glide, not away, but into her—was there in her features without still being visible.

She walked slowly on. He heard her footsteps, how she limped slightly against the frozen gravel. It was forced upon him that he wanted to mean much to her, do everything that stood in his power, look after her, always be good to her. . . .

"I thought you knew. . . ." he said with suppressed ardour in his voice.

She looked away, across the water.

"I thought . . ."

He wanted to take her hand, but she moved away, over to the quay. When he followed her she shook her head. He wanted to speak—but she laid her hand on his arm, almost pleadingly.

They went on in silence. He was breathing more quickly and looked straight ahead. His temples were burning.

"What a lot of gulls," she said gaily. "How beautiful they are, don't you think?"

"Yes—very."

They were approaching a little park which was empty of people. Dusk had glided in under the trees. He stopped in front of her, stood looking at her face. Her eyes met his, frank and yet shy, as only hers could be.

Then he kissed her—gently, as though in passionate reverence. She let it happen, but her lips were closed. They felt quite cool from the evening air.

He looked into her inquiringly, searchingly, his arms still around her. In her eyes was a deep gravity. Nothing reproachful, only great gravity. And he, too, felt something rise up inside himself by way of a mute answer. It was as if they had met and had understood each other.

There was no longer any quay. The water lapped against the shore, flowing past close by. Otherwise there was not a sound. Only the even roar of the city where the lights had been lit and up on the heights were merging with the last pale daylight. The rows of lights came on along the quays, but over the expanse of water it was getting darker. They walked in under the trees in silence.

He could just make her out beside him. In here it was already almost dark. They walked as though alone, far away from inhabited parts, in some other clime. Only the noise of the current came dully through the darkness and the clinking of the ice floes as they bumped together out there.

He stopped by a solitary lamp-post and looked at her. The face seemed pale; the isolated glow was like a halo round her. . . .

He wanted to bend down—but didn't—released her tenderly. . . . They walked again into the darkness.

"Why . . ." he whispered with bated breath.

"No. . . ."

He took her hand—pressed it hard, gently—hoping for an answer—her answer. . . .

"You know—it wouldn't . . .

"What?"

"Wouldn't be—true. . . ."

"Yes, yes," he whispered.

They were silent, walked close beside each other. Out in the darkness a sloop glided past with a fiery-red lantern, vanished into the mist.

Half-imperceptibly, she guided them along side paths back toward the city. The tram bells could be heard; away between the trees there was a flash in the frozen overhead wires.

They began talking. About everything which they had not had time to talk about yet. There was a great deal. She would ask what did *he* think? Yes, that's what she had thought. Was that right? She seemed glad and happy to be walking like this, talking to him about things which otherwise perhaps she kept to herself. Her voice took on all her rich warmth in its attempt to express what she wanted to say, how she felt, so that he would understand properly. When they chanced to look at each other now and then, her glance deepened and gleamed with thoughtful joy.

At last they had almost reached her door. She stopped and said that he might not come any farther.

He took her hand. Her cheeks had a brighter colour, a slight flush after the walk. There was no need for her to exert herself so much, for her to insist on doing so. Though it didn't really hurt her. And it made her even more beautiful, more wonderful. She was radiant—but a little distrait. . . . Her lips moved slightly with this floating smile —her smile. . . .

He could not see her like this—and part, just part—from this face, so close to him—and yet not close. . . . He kissed her—felt the shape of her lovely mouth, firm and cool. It was as if he had kissed her beauty itself. As if she had given him her soul to kiss.

She looked at him without a word—sadly, happily? Impossible to say. But wasn't she asking him to go—yes, yes, he was going. Tore himself from her image. . . .

She walked lingeringly along the street—into the vestibule, took the lift. Looked at her face in the mirror, gravely—stroked back her hair slightly from one temple just as the lift got up.

Dinner was just served, she had to go straight in. Her old mother was already there, a little, white-haired woman with small, fine features and with the same eyes as herself.

"What nice pink cheeks you have, my girl," she said as they sat down.

"Do you think so? Yes, it's such lovely weather."

"Oh, do you think so, and I thought it felt so raw."

After dinner she had to sit and read aloud while the old woman played patience. When it started to come out, she had to make a little pause. Then they sat talking for a while, as usual. Later in the evening she played Mozart and something else, something that Daddy had liked to hear. That was the Sunday ritual. Then they said good-night, kissing each other on the cheek.

She went to her room. Sat down to read but left the book lying in her lap, open too far ahead, where the pages had not yet been cut. Looked in front of her with large eyes, vacantly. . . .

Then she smiled, a strange, painful little smile—caught sight of her image far away in the mirror and put her hand to her hair, pushed it up a trifle at the sides—patted it into place, critically. Adjusted the cushion behind her and leaned slowly back. The light fell on her upturned face.

The mouth was half-open, there was a moist gleam on her teeth. She remained sitting for a long time.

At last she picked up the book, intending to read. Turned back the pages, cut them. But let it sink again. . . . Caught her glance over in the mirror. . . .

She went over and sat down in front of it, with her elbows on the dressing-table; passed her hand lightly over her eyebrows and back over her temples; raised the slender brows so that the eyes widened. Her irises had small, yellowish flecks which lent a golden touch to the dark rings; the pupils were large and quite black now in the light.

She got up, her gaze lingering searchingly in the mirror. Looked around the familiar room, went and put the book back.

She got undressed, put on pyjamas. Massaged her face, removed the cream. Put on a thin layer of another cream for the night. Put out the light. Lay listening to the faint rumble from the city and to her heart beating. Turned over to go to sleep. On the other side, as she usually lay.

Her leg ached slightly from all the exertion. It didn't matter. She could walk any distance when she felt like it. It wasn't that. It was rather tiring, didn't bother her otherwise.

From her manner the next time they met, the two of them might always have been in the habit of meeting— now they had their time to themselves again. When they had got away from people into their solitude and his face had taken on its dark, passionate expression, she gave him her mouth to kiss, took him to her as hers. She clung to him, held him fast, her mouth hot and open.

It came so suddenly that it almost bewildered him.

He stammered out his love—a few vehement, incoherent words, pressed her close to him. And she answered in a whisper, with her lips near his mouth, her warm breath entering into him, that she loved, loved him. . . .

They were intoxicated, confused. . . . The whole evening they were in ecstasy.

He called in at the office for a while and dictated one or two letters. Then he went again.

He couldn't sit shut in up there. And there was no need for him to sit there, either. Anyone could do what he did. It was as mechanical and uninspiring as anything could be. Orders, deliveries, telephone calls, correspondence. . . . The same machinery was started every morning and stopped at five. What was *he* needed for? Nothing. And after all, it was his brother who managed the business, who had the final say.

Only because he was supposed to sit there, because he belonged there. It was something he was born to, had heard about from childhood—the firm, the firm, business —nothing else.

How he burned inside with longing—to get away, far away. . . . He knew not to what.

Yes, he knew. . . . To that which was something to *live* for, really to live and exist for. . . .

Here time rushed ahead, unresting, without a breathing-space. Busy with a thousand different things, everything essential, absolutely *essential*. One's whole existence filled with a thousand small things, chopped up into seconds, tiny-tiny, into innumerable small *nows*. An existence filled with oneself, with one's occupation with oneself—mech-anical, unflagging—generation after generation, as life is so apt to be. Life which fundamentally is always sufficient unto itself, and gives human beings a few years in which to live. A few seconds, a few years. . . .

But within us the soul cries out, calls to us. . . .

Cries out for *its* life.

For a fire in which to burn—just *one*. A single flame in which to rise up and proclaim itself. Wants to exist. And wants to become *one*. *One*. . . .

It is scarcely audible. For it calls so *quietly*. Calls as with its silence—is noticed by not being noticed—burns by not burning.

Our soul—forsaken, cowed—by ourselves.

Yes—how empty and poor his life was. Comfortable in its seeming activity, its everlasting preoccupation with—what? Nothing. And his inner self? Wasn't he rootless, merely driven by his feelings and by his gnawing unease—this unease which was all he had really. Otherwise he was no good. Just worthless—useless, unnecessary to everyone, everywhere. . . . Belonged nowhere. Had no *home*. *That* was it—he had no home at all—anywhere.

Yes, he was poor, poor. Right up till *now*. *Now*.

Until *this* had happened.

Yes, he loved her, loved her. . . .

How wonderfully great to be able to feel like that! Feel his love for her—no bounds, no questions. Merely as a deep, deep breath—of liberation. Of fullness, of happiness.

Yes, he loved her. He knew it. He exulted at this glorious, great certainty. Something inside him had been transformed. Something had awakened, risen as though from a coma—become so alive, present in him. And filled up all emptiness—all, all.

It was as if his soul had been allowed to wake up, to live, at last—live for something—for *her*. He felt its reverent expectation within him—every moment—reverence, expectation—yes, yes . . . he went about as though keeping vigil.

It was great love. It must be, the greatest of all.

Another person to be fond of, really, dearly. To devote oneself to entirely. To treat tenderly and be good to. To support. . . .

How strange—he had had no idea of this before. Not until now. Now that it was reality.

No, love never comes as we think, always differently, with something special, something we had not expected. . . . He had thought of it in general terms as something delightful and mighty which would take hold of him, lift him up into its spheres—make him so exultingly happy!

We know nothing of the mystery. Of *passion*. . . .

Of that which cannot exult, which is too deep down in us merely to become anything like joy—what is called joy. We know nothing of love's mood of destiny, pain. . . .

No. . . .

And yet it was just this which made everything so exalted and grand, raised it to such purity and sublimity. Just this —which gave something he had never before felt with a woman—the longing for a human being, for someone else's innermost self. . . .

Yes, he loved her.

Thought of her—of his bird—huddled in his hand—the trembling heart. . . . Stroked softly, softly—felt the broken wing—

Yes, yes . . . their love had been born in pain, in sorrow, in what was heavy and grievous. With wings which did not want to bear them out into the storm, but which were going to bear them, which *must*—which would be forced to lift them upward, *upward*—higher, still higher—in spite of all, in spite of all. . . .

That was how he had always imagined love, dark, fraught with destiny. . . . There was nothing strange to him about it, he did not recoil. It was all so familiar to him. He had lived in this atmosphere in his dreams—had sought it out, been drawn, sucked toward it—unresistingly. . . . Only he had not imagined any particular reason. No. . . . That would be in love itself, perhaps in passion's almost agonizing excess. . . .

But in what he was now meeting the pain was real, had a cause.

Yes. And yet . . .

He saw the meaning of it. He *understood*.

Understood as he had been unable to do before. Perhaps that was the change in him, just that. That all he had dreamed and thought had come to meet him as reality—pain, happiness, sweetness and torment—everything. Life itself had come to meet him.

And yet all he felt was calm, expectation. He went in reverent expectation of what was to come, what life chose to bring, where it was to lead him. He was *ready*. Went about in a secret ecstasy, with his face gentle and open, naked and defenceless as a lover's face is. Roamed the streets—restless—with eyes that saw and yet did not see what surrounded him. He met people, a stream of people, met no one—was far away. Was with *her*. Inside *himself*. Went about longing to hear her footstep—and to sit talking together again, as only *they* could—to hear her well-known step—longing for the time when they would meet. . . .

Yes, it was Love, the perfect love; that which is without thought. As the soul is without thoughts, merely is, existing in itself.

She came up for a while as usual. The lights were on in both rooms and the table laid with his meagre offering, as he called his arrangements of fruit and flowers—her favourite roses in a large bowl and mimosa which diffused its sweet scent. They talked about a concert they had been to the evening before, about Bach whom they both worshipped. That had been the best of all! What followed was unnecessary really, for Bach had everything, and in the highest form musical inspiration could attain. But they had to admit that there were others they were fond of almost equally perhaps, though just at present they were so taken up with Bach. . . . They had to admit that! They should be grateful for whatever they could enjoy, for anything at all in which they delighted. And for the fact that there was such a thing as music. What would life be like otherwise? Difficult to imagine, it would have been another kind of existence. The life we feel inside us has rhythm, music as part of its essence. In fact, we could imagine ourselves as capable of listening to the *melos*, the secret rhythm of our inner self—imagine that life could be heard—if we possessed such a sense. Or—perhaps—if we did not have our senses to disturb us, distract us the whole time. We don't know to what extent our senses may also blunt, coarsen us, inure us to their strong stimulation; nor what we might perhaps divine if it were still for once. Perfectly still. . . .

He went over and sat beside her on the couch. Took her hand. They sat looking at each other. Then he kissed her, bending her slowly back.

"Darling. . . ."

"Oh. . . ."

She caressed his head, drew it down to her, clung to his lips with hers. He grew hot from the contact, from the close scent of her skin, seized her shoulders and held her beneath him. But she forced herself up, pushed him away, her hands shielding her from his deep, ardent gaze. . . . "Later, later —some time. . . ." she whispered. He looked at her darkly, beseechingly. But she shook her head. Put out her lips, half in reproach and half in consolation. . . . Then she put her arms around his neck and covered his mouth with light, caressing kisses, merely caressed it softly with hers. . . . He gasped and forced her down, held her, bared her shoulders, and then almost her breasts, embraced her bare body.

Suddenly she changed, fought to get free—to move her arms, twisted away with the strength of despair. At last she bit his hand so that he had to let her go. Sat up trembling. Then she burst out crying.

"Arna?" He tried to talk to her, caress her. . . . She merely cried, pushed him away.

"But Arna. . . . It's only because . . . Arna! You must know that."

She held the wet, crumpled handkerchief to her eyes. "You only care for me in that way," she sobbed.

"I! I do? How can you say that?"

She raised her head and stopped crying. Squeezed the handkerchief.

"It seems like it," she said.

"How can you think that—and after all we have had together. . . . And you say that I only want to—you ought to know it's not possible."

She looked down at the floor where he stood, without raising her eyes to his; sat looking dry-eyed.

"Why do you say such silly things?" he said.

He knew that she was doing him an injustice and was overcome by a feeling of bleak dejection, wherever it came from. Went over to the window. Neither said anything. The silence was tense and painful. He began walking up and down.

Then he went over to her, however. Took her head between his hands. Stroked her hair tenderly, gently.

"Arna. . . . You know quite well that I love you. . . . You *do* know, don't you? Arna? I love you more than I can say, than I can explain."

She looked at him shyly, guardedly and fervently. And he took her and kissed her. He didn't quite recognize her mouth after the tears; it was so loose. He caressed her until she was quite still.

There was something timorous about her. But she was warm and soft from having cried, and cuddled up to him. Put her arm around his neck and began kissing him over and over again with her wet face to his. Looked at him. . . . Her eyes dilated, as though to open for his. They smiled at each other—she wanly and breathlessly. Then she slid right up against him, holding herself taut, clinging to him and panting. . . . He fondled her legs which lay quivering against him. The right one felt a shade more slender than the other—he withdrew his hand. Kissed her quickly, tenderly, and raised her up. Smoothed her hair, which was all rumpled, stroked it back from her forehead. Helped her with it. She gave a slightly forced smile and moved her head away. Combed her hair back with a few vigorous strokes. Tidied her dress.

"Would you like some fruit?" he said.

"No, thank you."

After a moment he himself took a French pear and peeled it.

"Are you sure you won't have something?" he asked. "They're excellent."

"No, my dear, I don't feel like it."

He went on eating, gave his mind to it.

There was a blank—only a slight scraping against the plate, and the glint of the ceiling light for a moment. Seemed to take a long time for him to finish. They sat there in silence.

"Give me a cigarette," she said.

He went and got them, gave her a light. Put out ash-trays, which he had forgotten. The rumble of the trams could be heard from below, but faintly, from away in the side streets.

She pulled up her legs on the couch, tucked a cushion under her and stretched out, settled down until she lay comfortably on her back. Lay humming softly, looking up at the ceiling. Stretched out her arm and lay slowly tapping the cigarette with her finger. Went on doing it. . . . Laid her head back on the cushion and smiled to herself, as though she had just thought of something. Raised herself as if she were not quite comfortable.

Suddenly he threw himself over her and tore open her clothes.

And she let him come, take her, bury his heated face in her breasts, but without touching him. Lay there with the cigarette out over the table—dropped it on the plate. Until she gradually wakened—slowly like an animal which gets up without there being any sign of the quarry's approach— clung tightly around him, soft and quiet, without a sound; all that was heard was a groan.

Inside him he exulted, exulted. He loved her! Loved her! Yes! Yes! It was true. He *knew* it. He felt it inside him in glowing happiness. Dragged his mouth across her breasts as if he would swallow them—across her, his beloved. Seized her, against him, she, she. . . . There was no doubt—only inexpressible, dizzy happiness—with her. . . . He looked into her eyes which lost their gaze. . . . And her smile—painful, broken—*her* smile which he recognized so well in the midst of his ecstasy—he kissed it, kissed her very pain—because it was *she, she*—whom he loved. . . . And when she put the hot tip of her tongue into his mouth. . . . Yes, yes! He loved *her!*

At the same time as they got married, early in the spring, he retired from the firm and had nothing more to tie him here at home. The wedding was very quiet, with only his brother and her old mother present. In the evening they left for abroad.

Abroad, away—the two of them. The train rushed through the night. They listened, twined together. . . . Alone! Nothing else to exist for any longer but each other. Nothing in the world but themselves, their love! They couldn't imagine it, not *properly*—to be able to live only for that, for one another. A whole life together. Given to the beloved, dedicated to love, utterly, completely. As it *should* be. As we dream of it, as all long for it deep down, long to make their hearts come true. . . .

The countryside outside the window was hardly visible, although they had dimmed the light in their compartment. Only the stars. Pale. Straying in the windowpane that was dripping with damp. It was like a dream—a waking dream. Their life beginning, mysteriously. . . . They were carried away together into the night. . . . .

Far, far away to a strange land, to unknown people, to hide themselves with their happiness!

To beauty, the South! Perfection.

They passed through towns — on, away — stopped at places where they had each been on their own at some time, but which now seemed entirely new to them in their happiness. Strolled in the crowd, the strange crowd in which their voices were lighter than all others. Went on. Left. Went on. Until the Alps sank behind them and the country spread out, seeming to bathe in perpetual sun.

It was not just sunny, a fine day, as at home. But something perpetual, something that *was* like that. Which lay under the bare sky, open and naked. Which was the land of Day. The plain seemed to them adorned for a festival with the grapevines wreathing in garlands between the trees as far as the eye could see, mile after mile, blossoming trees, as in eternal spring. And when the mountains began again they lay sunny and clear, resting in light. Rose higher and higher, with aged towns and villages on the summits, lifted as though in rapture toward heaven, in ecstasy over life. As if the very earth raised itself in fervour and lifted its life in carefree gifts toward the heights. It was all awake, real, close. It was the land of Day. Until the country sloped down once again. Breathed freely, calmly, reverently. In thoughts, solemnity. Perfect peace. Opened up like a soul, naked and pure. . . .

Tuscany—Tuscany—with the vines bursting into leaf over the hills, on the black, almost charred stems. The slopes grey with olives, with gentle, Biblical greenery, aged, faded by thousands of years of sun. The olive, mother of trees, which has grown grey in the earth's service. Cypresses rose up in the distance, apart, as at sacred places. Stone

pines lifted their crowns, floating, like spirits of the air.
Life, death. Death and life.

Tuscany. . . .

It seemed to them in their boundless happiness more
austere than they had thought. Very grave. Almost dark
in fact. But its beauty was nevertheless far too great for one
really to be weighed down by it. They were moved—freed.
As beauty always seems to free. At last only frees. . . .

Yes, they were almost dizzy with joy. When they had
reached Florence! Joy at being there! Went about in an
ecstasy of happiness—which at the same time felt curiously
still, like devotion. Roamed the narrow streets between
the palaces which lay there solemn and mighty. Almost
gloomy. Read the marble tablets at the street corners with
quotations from Dante. . . .

Dante, Beatrice. . . .

They pressed close to each other. Walked down along
the Arno, silent, devout. With shining eyes. . . .

Vita nuova. . . . New life through love. . . .

Yes, which for them . . .

Until they looked at each other—saw that they thought
the same. Gave a smile—Glided caressingly in between
each other's fingers, into the beloved's hand, lightly, im-
perceptibly, made each other hot. . . .

They were in the churches, where there was so much to
see and enjoy, stood together under the shadowy arches in
bliss. They saw art, experienced all the glory and splendour
that has been created by the mind of man, perfectly, for all
time. Found their way to secluded sanctuaries, to incon-
ceivable treasures through lanes and passages where people
sat eating their bread in the doorway and the brazier
glowed inside in the dirty darkness. They lived as in a
constant ecstasy.

After a time they moved up to Fiesole, on the slope
toward the valley, toward the Arno. Rested, in sunshine,
among roses. Flowering clematis and wisteria climbed over

the walls, flowing over from the wealth of the innumerable
gardens; the villas lay light and open in the spring air with
the loggias full of drowsy scents. It was stupefying. They
felt the breath of the South strike against them with its
violent, flaming heat. Dry days which made life transparent as glass and kept the body taut in an enervating
vigil. In the evenings they walked along the path around
the hills of Fiesole and lingered in the grove of stone pines
on the south side where the scent of resin still steamed under
the trees after the sun had gone down behind the mountains
and the lights began to appear down in Florence, all along
the valley. Dusk was falling and they hurried home before
the path grew too dark. Made their way through the
garden, into the hall and up to their room, without putting
on the light. Opened the windows to the cool of the night.
Silent, beside each other. Were drawn into their love, their
passion, overwhelmed, without words.

The frogs croaked down in the valley. The fireflies
darted outside in the night, came into the room like floating
sparks.

It was sweet, sweetest of all to lie still, beside each other,
waiting, as in holy waiting, while love arched its temple,
its holy night over them—incomprehensibly big. . . . Space
only deepened more and more the longer they looked into
it. Their eyes were filled with a wonder of all wonders. . . .
It was like a solemn festival, a celestial temple ceremony
at which they were present. . . .

He bent down over her in unspeakable, trembling happiness. . . . Put on the light in order to see her, in order to see
her before passion swept them up into itself, into its de-
lirium. She lay there with her arms under her head, the
small breasts contracted, hardly noticeable, like a boy's.
Taut and shining like a blade, waiting for him to come.
Resisted, didn't want to, caused him to grow more violent.

Outside was Tuscany with quivering stars above the
hills, with gleaming lights rising toward them, up over the

heights; one couldn't tell which was sky and which was earth.

The days slipped past, large, clear, like pearls lost from a hand; caressed as they were lost, as they glided away. Costly, priceless—to be filled, filled with a single feeling of rejoicing! Mighty, urgent. Glowing through one's soul, one's limbs, like an omnipotent fire. The joy of living, of loving. Of existing on a loved, wide-open earth.

Down there Florence spread itself out for them every morning in lavish splendour, sunny and extensive, with the cathedral and the campanile at its heart. With its palaces and churches, its cupolas and towers. The whole valley with the winding ribbon of the Arno stretched out for them when they looked out—in a single vista. Right up by San Miniato they could make out Michelangelo's David, naked and gigantic, gazing into the distance like an imperious young heathen god. It was overwhelming. Pregnant and rich like a hymn. And when in the stillness of Sunday morning the bells began to ring down there—all the bells of Florence, San Lorenzo's, Santa Croce's, Santa Maria Novella's, Santissima Annunziata's—and above them all those of the campanile with their clear notes raised up to heaven—they stood in silence. Mute. In wonder at this song of praise in the sun, through the valley. . . . Round about lay the countryside, dark, solemn and seeming to listen. Bare as a face and unapproachable. As though sunk into itself.

They could not tear themselves away from this countryside which had so captivated their souls. Lingered week after week, longer than they had intended. Not until they thought it was beginning to get too hot did they leave and move up to the mountains. Up to the lakes under the Alps, in a gentle coolness from the eternal snows. Pretended they were in the North among meadows with buttercups and forget-me-not, only larger, more lush than they were used to. With bilberries on the edge of the forest where they lay watching the peasant women cut the hay with a sickle on the steep slopes and the men carry it home in large cocks on their backs like heavily laden animals. They led a free and glorious summer life in this magnificent scenery, among a fine and cordial people. Sound, frank mountain-dwellers who were content with their simple lot. More often than not jovial and gay. When you met them they always beamed, even worn-out old men and women, bent from all they had borne in their day. The countryside had nothing oppressive and gloomy about it either, as in a Scandinavian tract of similar wildness. Always had an exhilarating effect on one, like a festival. It was huge and yet gentle, approachable. At night, not long before sunrise, they would sometimes wake to the sound of a horn up in the mountains, hear the young people going home toward the village; they could tell from the sound how the road twisted slowly down through the valley.

They had a long, unforgettable time here. In the late summer, on one of the last days, they went for a farewell walk up into the forest, higher up than usual, in a direction where they should have a particularly good view. The weather was at its loveliest now, these days when the warmth had a tang which made it infinitely easy to breathe. The trees had already begun to turn, to take on autumn's profuse colours; the chestnuts were waiting to be harvested; the walnut trees burned down on the slope like bright yellow torches. As they walked along they revelled in all this glory and in breathing the clean air. The path was steep but they took it slowly so that it would not be too strenuous. When they reached the top the view was indeed enchanting. They stood together gazing, without a word spoken. With their senses brimming, as they do when you stand looking out over country which you must leave and in all likelihood will not see again. Filled with a strange, tugging happiness but also with melancholy.

Behind them was a grassy glade where they sat and

rested for a while. There was a small hut of unhewn stone, the kind used for sheltering the sheep at night but far too small to be used for such. Dilapidated, in one corner it had half fallen in. Over the entrance a cross had been painted in whitewash. When they opened the rickety door and peeped in they saw that it was a chapel. By the far wall was an altar and over it was a yellowed newspaper spread out as a cloth, its edges cut in zigzags as one does with shelf-paper in a pantry. Against the wall was a dusty little post-card of the Madonna and in front of it some flowers in a broken glass. The simplicity of it all moved them, especially the altar cloth, and they stayed there for a long time in the semi-darkness. If the wall had not collapsed it would have been almost dark.

When they came out they both thought they had seldom been in a temple which so disposed them to reverence. And what a glorious position! Right down below wound the lake, deep blue and with steep shores which in this light gleamed like mother-of-pearl.

But they must go back now. They didn't want to hurry, and if they were to take their time going down and get back to the hotel for dinner they had better be making a start. Going down was actually more of a strain for her foot, though he helped her at the difficult places. When they got home it was aching slightly, not enough to worry her, but she lay down and rested for a while all the same.

A day or two later they went away. Returned, strength-ened, to the South, to all that was still awaiting them. Passed Tuscany, which lay there burned and scorched and perhaps did not make the same impression on them as the first time, but a very strong one even so. They visited other places now, Lucca, Pisa and the austere, medieval Siena, adding new experiences to their former ones. Then down into Umbria, the land of religious ecstasy, where the roads between the mountains have something holy about them because St Francis has walked them. Imbued themselves in this world, in Assisi's jumble of churches, monasteries, monk-filled streets, and made a pilgrimage out to the place in the wilderness where he received the stigmatization. Went on soon afterward to Rome and stayed there for some time. Still farther, down to the Gulf of Naples, sunny Sorrento where summer yet lingered.

Their life had really become one long festival. They couldn't believe it was true that one could live like this! So fully, so richly and gloriously.

Now it was like a new summer for them. With sun and flowers. And the sea was there, just below their window. It was the first time they really saw the Mediterranean, lived by it and heard it break in long, invisible breakers against the shore. The gulf widened, always just as blue, with the rocky island of Ischia farthest out, with Naples and Vesuvius and at night the endless string of lights along the coast.

It was a place for happiness, for lovers. And they were intoxicated by happiness. They felt like heathens in all this earthly beauty, perfection, but at the same time filled with love's solemnity, their hearts trembling from their great wonder as from the mighty peal of an organ. Their love seemed to embrace everything, both heaven and earth. It was like a huge instrument on which to play. Carefree and sacred, playful and yet always just as full-toned and deep. Their whole existence was like a carefree game to the sound of solemn organ music.

They couldn't grasp that a feeling could so penetrate their entire being, unite two people so completely to each other. Although each day gave them so many new impressions, they really only existed for each other, and everything around them at last had a value only because they saw it together. How poor it all would have been if they had not done so! The wealth came from their love; through it they were able to get so much out of everything, steep themselves in all they saw. Their souls broadened and became receptive as never before, but at the same time almost absent, fleeting, thoughtful, each living only in its own world.

Here they threw themselves into the motley tumult of the South, with the gay, responsive people who threw all care to the winds. Wallowed like animals in existence, as one must do here.

They had discovered the real South and fallen in love with it. Were enticed even farther down, to Sicily, Taormina, Girgenti. . . . With Greek temples, blossoming almond trees, Etna's snowcap shimmering in the distance. . . . All one could desire of earthly beauty. Until in the early spring they went north again.

They found that this was just the very way it suited them to live. They were independent and wanted to be, to feel, fully independent. They had little need of people and social life. They were sufficient unto themselves, their love and happiness.

They continued to stay abroad. Only came home sometimes for the summer and once, reluctantly, in the middle of winter because her mother died. Often during the season they lived on the Riviera, but away from the crowds and noise, the everlasting carnival life, masquerades, *batailles de fleurs*, which was nothing for them. They preferred quietude and a certain solitariness. They both had a leaning to this, and what meant most of all to them perhaps was scenery. This was what they sought here, too, and the lovely climate.

Imposing scenery was always a source of refreshment to them if ever they felt tired or bored. Perhaps that was why they travelled so much. It became at last a need for them to travel, not to be bound too much to anything hard and fast.

They had their life, that was all. Became absorbed in the very existence which they shared. Lived for each other in an unusually harmonious way.

They were happy. Life had become perfect. As they had imagined.

They were at home one summer after several years, were staying by the sea. Sat one afternoon down on the beach sunbathing. Some small children, three- and four-year-olds, were bathing not far away, came in and played, rolled about in the sand and splashed out into the water again.

"It's lovely today. The sun's really hot," he said.

She nodded.

"That sailboat hasn't moved the whole time. They'll have to take to the oars if they want to get in. But I expect it's only out with holiday-makers. . . . Look, now they have to start rowing!"

"Yes."

"But you're not looking," he laughed.

"Aren't I? Oh yes."

They sat on for a while longer. She seemed to be wool-gathering.

"Let's go," she said, getting up.

"Why? All right, if you want to."

They walked in toward the sunny grey rocks, a kind of path which almost wasn't there at all. Some little way from the shore they lay down on a knob of rock from where they had a view right out to sea. The small rocky islands lay smooth and shining, low and polished by the sea. Farthest out there was a blue glitter.

"There's wind out there," he said, pointing. "Just over there off Bullareskären. And out by Hovö there's quite a breeze."

She made no reply but looked for a moment where he was pointing. Glanced down at some heather which had taken root in a crevice at her feet. It seemed impossible that there should be any earth there. It came up out of a mere crack.

"What are you thinking of?" he said, taking her hand.

"Nothing."

"Yes, there's something. . . ."

She lay moving a blade of grass slowly across the smooth slab of rock and looking down, absently.

"Don't you sometimes think it's strange," she said at last—"strange that we haven't any children?"

"We? Yes. . . ." He looked at her wonderingly. "Yes, it is. . . . But I thought — well, that we didn't want any. That's what we used to say, that it was best like that."

"No . . . we didn't say that, did we?"

"Yes. . . . You know we did. . . . Before, in the beginning, when we talked about it once. And before we got married, too. . . ."

"Oh yes, then. That was different."

"Do you want to, Arna? I didn't think you did."

He took her hand again.

"You've never even hinted. . . ."

She made no reply, lay with averted glance.

"Every woman wants to," she said presently. "She feels there's something missing otherwise."

He stroked her hand gently.

"Do you often think about it?"

"Yes—I suppose I do. . . ."

"A lot?"

"Quite a lot. . . ."

He moved closer to her and took her gently by the shoulders. She looked down and fingered the buttons of his jacket.

"I think it's so strange that a love like ours does not give us a child."

"Yes. But it's not because of love."

"No—but I think it should be."

"Yes, that would be right. . . . It would be the most natural if it were so."

She was silent. Looked out to sea with eyes that were dry and rather dull.

"What is the reason then?" she said.

"Well, dear—you know just as well as I do. That is to say—how is one to know—one can't always tell."

She lay down on her back with her hands to her temples.

"It's my fault," she said.

"But darling—Why should it be?"

He bent over her, stroked her hair, her cheek and neck.

"Why do you think about it, Arna dear? We're evidently not meant to have children—and we can't help that, either you or I. . . . But we have each other. *That* means a lot. Doesn't it?"

"Yes."

They were silent for a long time. He sat up, gazed out to sea, but held her tightly by the hand. It felt slack in his; she lay stretched out beside him with her head against the rock.

"I expect I'm the one with something wrong," she said.

"No, Arna—how can you say that?" He turned to her almost violently; looked into her wide, rather tired eyes.

It hurt him to see her. He knew that he was not the one at fault, for once in his youth he had made a girl pregnant. He caressed her gently, with tender affection; kissed her quickly so that the passers-by would not notice them. But lingered over her, by her face. Glided over her brow, stroked the soft hair back from it, could make out each little strand of hair in the fine skin.

"Listen—I think that two people who have no children can mean all the more to each other—something very special to each other. As we do. In that way they have their love to make up for what they have had to do without. Don't you think so, too?"

"Yes," she said. "I suppose so."

He watched her face. Slender and a little tense. The

complexion was pale, yet with that warm tinge which she had, and not at all sunburned; she never was.

"Let's go," she said.

"Don't you want to sit here, either?" he said with a smile.

"Yes—but we can take a little walk all the same."

They clambered down the rock to the path leading to the beach. Oh no, they could go inland instead. She thought it would be better.

They went for an hour's walk.

In the evening, when they had gone up to their room at the boarding house after supper and she was sitting on the sofa as she usually did, she said, "Halvdan—do you think it's because of me?"

"But my dear—with a thing like that it's impossible to tell. You know that. . . ."

She sat looking out of the window with the pale light in her eyes; folded her hands in her lap, which was not like her and which somehow did not quite suit her.

"You know it's because of me," she said.

"Nonsense! I haven't the faintest idea, darling. How could I?"

"But it's nearly always something wrong with the woman. I've heard that."

"Nearly always. Perhaps."

"Yes."

"But Arna, my dear, why should we talk about it? What's the use? Let's go out and sit on the balcony for a while. . . . Come and see how nice it is."

She came out slowly. The sea was calm and smooth between the countless skerries, with light colours after the sunset wafted into the bays toward the bare, grey land. The fjord in toward the east had grown dark, gone to rest, deep and clear, between its watchful hills.

It was a mild evening with no wind. They sat for a long time talking together of many things, as was their wont; he with his arm on the back of her chair. He took her slender white fingers and let them rest between his.

When they went to bed he looked at her, kissed her with sudden ardour, held her to him. But she shook her head, said good-night. She felt rather tired, it had been quite a long walk.

Next day the weather was not so good. But during the afternoon it cleared and the evening was soft and mild, more than any previously. They lay down by the shore long after the others had gone.

Small golden clouds melted into the sky in the west, turned for a while into blood-red streaks and then vanished as if they had never been. That was as dark as it got now.

They sat there in silence, watching the approach of the summer night. It struck him that she had grown more reticent of late. Perhaps during the last year or two. More reserved, a little secretive. But people don't notice this so much when the change is gradual and they are always together.

She picked some flowers that were around her in the dusk, two kinds which were growing right down by the edge of the sand—a small pink one and one that was white, with a calyx like a bell. Arranged them and sat holding them in her lap.

"What kind of flowers are those—do you know what they're called?" he asked.

"No—I don't know. They're quite pretty."

"Yes. One thinks that about all flowers here, however unassuming they look."

"Here they call them shore boy and shore girl," she said, rearranging the nosegay. "But I expect they have some other name."

"Yes—I expect they have."

When they went home she took them with her. He kissed her. And they walked on. He took her arm under his. Outside where they lived they stopped for a moment as usual, stood there because of the view. The open sea was to the west. It was a shame to go in on such an evening; they just stood there.

"You shouldn't think about it so much, Arna," he said.

She gave him a little smile.

The days were long. They kept away from the beach, where people were always coming and going. And they preferred to bathe elsewhere, by themselves.

"But if it's the woman's fault they say it's possible to do something," she said once as they lay resting after their swim.

"Yes—so they say."

"Did you know that?"

"I've heard about it. It's supposed to be so in some cases."

"I—I don't think it's like that with me."

"Oh—why not? Why shouldn't you just as well think so? And it's probably quite a simple matter."

She made no reply; sat for a while.

"Do you think it can be helped, Halvdan?"

"What is one to think? It's hard to say. It all depends."

"Yes. Of course. It does. Perhaps I'd only be told it can't be."

"We must be prepared for that, too. But why have such an idea at the outset? There's no reason for it."

She sat without a word.

"It's quite possible. . . . Indeed it is."

They talked no more about it now, but returned to it again. And even if she didn't mention it for some time he knew that she couldn't get it out of her mind. Tormented herself with it.

It grieved him always to see her like this. He said that it was better for her to know definitely. Began to inspire her with hope—that something could surely be done about it.

Perhaps it could be put right quite easily. Why shouldn't it be? She ought to find out for certain; it was surely much better than this. She thought so too. He knew of a doctor in town who was the most suitable to consult.

It ended by his persuading her and at last she went off.

When she returned and he met her down by the boat, she was embarrassed and would hardly speak. But there was a radiance from within her; he could feel it although she pretended it was nothing.

Up in their room she threw her arms around his neck and her eyes filled with tears. It had been as he thought. A simple case, the doctor had said, and wise of her to come.

"You see! I was right, you see."

They were overjoyed, had a wonderful day, the happiest they could remember for a long time. They went for a walk, close beside each other, were down on the beach and watched the bathers—all the sunburned children who were enjoying themselves, living in the sea almost from morning to night.

And despite the life all around them in the sunshine they felt quiet, rather far away. So filled with solemnity, with what was *theirs*.

They had a glass of wine with dinner as though they were celebrating their own secret festival by themselves. He nodded to her over the glass, gaily and yet seriously. Saw her eyes shine with their former deep glow, keep him with her. He was glad to have regained her.

The time that followed was strange in its happiness— expectation and happiness. Hope and at the same time uncertainty—it felt so curiously alive. Everything lived within them and around them in a special way. Everything had a calm warmth and intimacy which communicated itself to them. They went for walks, down by the sea and inland where the rocks were swept bare by the wind, with heather and bog myrtle in the clefts and bramble bushes here and there by the edges. And a little farther in oaks, buffeted by the wind, creeping along the rock like shrubs, growing together to shield each other from the blast. Sometimes in a sheltered crevice there was flowering honeysuckle to which they were led by the wafts of scent.

They lived in everything, with everything, as lovers can do. Were both carefree and braced by their happiness, and that seemed to make it even greater. The whole of life was braced—and yet mild as a summer evening. When they came to each other the sleeping land lay there outside, barren and familiar, like something staunch, and the breeze from the sea puffed the curtain gently into the semi-dark room.

She had a tenderness as never before, a different, maternal tenderness which felt infinite. Which felt strangely sweet after the ardour with which they had once loved each other. Deep and intimate, and with something hidden, unspoken. When he satisfied her she hardly let it be noticed, merely held her breath. It had a mystic effect in some way.

Time passed. Summer drew to an end. They never spoke of that which was in their minds, around which her thoughts must constantly have centred. She seemed to go about in a gentle trustfulness—not real belief, but something in which she wanted to exist, let herself sink down more and more. It was as if she wanted only to keep humble and quiet, and completely carefree; wanted to try to be so. Attached herself, warm and safe, to him and their love.

People began to leave. It grew emptier on the beach, the promenade and down by the casino. But it had nothing to do with them.

She was gay and happy. Yes, it seemed as though she really felt so.

Until one day she confided to him that she *hoped*—only hoped—for it was hardly possible. It couldn't be.

But one or two things pointed to it all the same. It might well be the case. He thought so, too.

Yes, she *believed*—something inside her also seemed to tell her that it *was* so. She couldn't be mistaken about it. She even thought she began to feel nausea, if it could really be due to that; it was not too early for it. He didn't know so much about that exactly. But it was quite likely.

The boarding-house began to empty; each day there were fewer people in the dining-room. They for their part had no thought of leaving. No plans at all for that matter. They lived at present only in this.

And these early autumn days—clear, bracing, with a sky so thin that it was really an inexpressible joy to breathe deeply. The hills gleamed with moisture in the cool sun-light and the sea had a greenish tinge right into the bays. Everything was at its most beautiful now, just now! There was no denying it. In this indescribable air. And the chilly water rustling like silk along their bodies when they bathed. They felt so exhilarated and so wonderfully light-hearted. Even if a little under par. For she actually felt rather seedy. But that, too, was nice, didn't matter. If she didn't always feel quite so well. She would come in pale and content after having been sick, laughingly rinse her mouth and look over at him meaningly, wet-eyed from the exertion.

There was no longer any doubt of how matters stood. None at all.

But now they were the only guests left in the boarding-house. They, too, must be thinking of going. Besides the place was closing down.

They didn't quite know what they would do. But of course there was no question of going abroad. They no longer would or could. Not in these circumstances naturally.

So it happened that after a time they found themselves back in their home town after having been away from it for so many years. And that they got themselves a flat, a real home. It gave them unexpectedly great pleasure to get it in order; to see again old, familiar things which had been in their families and which belonged to them—and to complement them with new, to choose beautiful things which went well together with the others, try to harmonize it all into a real whole. It gave them plenty to think of and ready play for their taste and personal discrimination. They found that they had a knack of coming across valuable things, which just suited them, in antique shops.

They were also glad to see the town again after such a long time. It was like something new. But as regards the people they felt rather out of it, they had grown away from them. They made hardly any new friends, not more than were absolutely necessary. They had each other.

And their home. For they had already grown really fond of it. It was already dear to them. It enclosed them with its tranquillity—they felt at home there from the first moment. They thought it was strange that the idea had not occurred to them long ago; that they roamed about for so long. They had really been quite restless.

She thought of the little corner room for the nursery. It faced south and was the sunniest of the smaller rooms. "It will be excellent, don't you think so?" Yes, it ought to be.

When they had really settled down she also started getting the little one's layette ready, though there was plenty of time. But she wanted to do everything herself and preferably by hand. Began with the unnecessary things, those that were really sweet and dainty. But then she got to work on diapers, covers and such like, sat perseveringly every day. Collected it all in piles; at last she had a whole shelfful in the linen cupboard. "But aren't you doing far too much?" he said. "Oh no. You just don't understand, darling. You need an awful lot."

She kept quite well under the circumstances. Their doctor was also satisfied with her. And it was a good thing she was in such good spirits. Well, why not? And they knew that it meant a lot for the child. She was rather tired, of course. But that was all part of it.

By degrees, as time passed, she felt the tiredness more. Toward the end of the winter. She was very swollen, unusually so perhaps, and it made her heavy and cumbrous and her feet troubled her. She had to lie down often, several times a day at last. But she only rested for a little while, for she mustn't get into the habit.

Otherwise everything ran its normal course. She suffered a lot from heartburn the whole time, but then most people do. She had nothing worse than what was normal. And there was nothing wrong with the albumen.

"He's evidently going to be a real little ruffian," he said, for she began to get more and more shapeless. In fact, she showed it in many ways. Her face was gaunt and wan, sallow up by the forehead. Her cheeks were sunken, her neck had also grown thin and drawn. "What a sight I look," she said, glancing into the mirror with her little smile. "Don't you think so, Halvdan?"

"Yes, you look awful," he said, scrutinizing her. She nodded in full agreement.

The last month was the worst. She kept lying down for the most part. It was too much to carry about, was too much of a strain on her leg; it was better for her if she just kept quiet. But she must move about if all was to go well. Be up and about as much as ever she could.

They went for a little walk together every day, were out for a while at least. It was spring now, too, and fine weather. Everywhere in the parks the trees were in leaf. They went for the same walks as during their very first time, along by the water, for they liked that best; he with her under his arm, on the side with the bad leg where she needed his support a little. They had to walk slowly, of course, but she managed quite well.

She tried to keep on with these walks right up to the last. It was not essential, though very good in one way. But she ought to take things more quietly. It was really painful to see her limping along like that with her burden. Despite the fact that he thought there was something sublime and lovely about it. He was really proud of her at the same time, of her condition.

But she was having far too bad a time, poor thing. He couldn't stop thinking about it, though she didn't want them to talk about it. She did, now, however—more than most.

It was almost a relief when the doctor, after an examination, wanted her to go into the nursing home. He was not quite satisfied with her heart and anyway it was just as well that he had her there. It might be any moment now.

At home it was strange and empty. Moving about in the rooms quite alone. But he was with her as often as he was allowed. Until one evening he received a telephone call to come at once. It had already begun.

He ran down the stairs and threw himself into a taxi.

He was not allowed to go in. Only outside in the corridor.

There was someone screaming most horribly. But it couldn't be she, for it wasn't at all her voice. Must be someone else who was also giving birth.

But—it must—be she! Couldn't be anyone else!

He asked. Yes, she was in there, the third door.

It was she—*Good God!*

It didn't even sound human. Was like nothing. It was something utterly unnatural. . . .

And then *she—she*! Oh good God. . . .

And it went on and on, the whole time the same, screech after screech, without ceasing, without a moment's break— until it grew slurred, more of a groan, and at last stopped.

A nurse came out.

"Is it over?" he asked.

"No, they have put her to sleep."

"She screamed again in there. . . ."

"Only lightly, and it hasn't acted yet."

"But can't they put her to sleep *properly*, so that she doesn't have to be tortured so terribly?"

"She's supposed to have a weak heart."

A weak heart, a weak heart, a rather weak heart— rather—Oh good Lord!

He clasped his hands. "Dear, dear God! Let it be all right, let it be all right!"

He could hear her breathing. Panting. It was no normal breathing. It sounded like some kind of pump. A hoarse pump. Not at all like a living being.

Yes, *rather* weak, rather—nothing to *worry* about. . . .

She started screaming again. Then was quiet once more. Only breathed. But that was almost worse, yes much worse. . . .

If only she survives it, if only she survives it. . . .

He walked up and down, up and down outside the door. Couldn't stand still for a moment.

An eternity passed.

It *was* a long, long time, too. He looked at the clock. Yes, and then *before*—it had begun long before. . . .

At last a nurse came out, must be the head nurse. He went toward her with a slack, inquiring face.

She shook her head.

"But how is it going? How is it going?" he asked.

She again shook her head.

"Badly. Very badly," she said.

He went white as a sheet. Fingered his hat—didn't know —know what—didn't . . .

The nurse had only come out to give an order. Went in again. He was standing by the door and caught a glimpse of the operating theatre with a strong light, she lying on

the table—the doctor had blood on him—blood everywhere, it steamed—several nurses holding her—looked as
if they were in the act of slaughtering her. . . .

Dear God!

He was seized with terror. Horror. Didn't know what he
could do—didn't know . . .

Dear God!

He wanted to go down on his knees—if that could save
her—if he prayed properly, properly for her—just that she
wouldn't die, that she wouldn't die—yes, he must pray
properly for her—he must—Now! Now at once!

But there was nowhere he could do it—not here in the
corridor, where nurses and visitors were passing all the
time—nowhere. . . .

At last he went into a lavatory, locked the door and
threw himself down on the floor. "Dear, gracious God—as
long as she doesn't die—help her—help us—grant that she
may *live*—all I have—the most precious thing I have on
earth—that she may be saved, can be saved—I shall
thank, thank Thee on my knees—if only she can live—
dear, dear God. . . ."

He got up, panting. Held his head. Brushed his knees
before going out.

There was no one in the corridor. And outside the door
there was not a sound. It was silent in there—quite silent.

He strained his ears . . . could hear nothing. Only the
doctor's voice once.

He drew a deep breath.

After a few minutes the head nurse came out.

"Is it—over?"

"Yes," she said.

"All right? Has it—gone—well?"

"Perhaps you can come in," she said. "I'll ask."

He was left outside.

Yes, he could come.

There was a reek of lysol and in the sharp light he was

at first almost blinded. He saw something bloody which a nurse was just covering up. Farther in on a stretcher she was lying. Pallid and lifeless. Like a dead person. But her chest was heaving violently. He bent over her. Kissed her, over and over again. She did not open her eyes. Seemed to be aware of nothing. As if she were asleep. They rolled her away on the stretcher.

"It was the only thing to do," the doctor said, pulling off his rubber gloves. "Had she not been so weak, and then this heart business, we'd have performed a Caesarian, you know. But it was unthinkable. In all probability she would never have come through it."

He breathed in relief. . . . "And now?" he said.

"Out of danger. If nothing unforeseen happens."

"Thank God for that. . . ."

"Yes. It was difficult. Very. And she won't survive anything like it again. That's my opinion."

"No, no—I understand."

He had washed and now came and shook hands.

"You must forgive me. I didn't want to tell you in advance how hard it was going to be. And it wouldn't have helped for you to have known it either, and perhaps have hinted it to her in some way."

"No, no, of course—I'm grateful to you. Grateful for everything. I know you've done *everything*. . . ."

"Yes, all that could be done. But it's just as well that things went as they did."

"Now she will sleep," he added. "It's no good your going in to her any more this evening, I think. But you ought to be here tomorrow when she wakes. Best if you're here then."

"Yes. Yes. Of course. Of course I shall be."

He thanked the doctor again warmly and all the nurses. Left the room. Stood again out there in the corridor. Took a deep breath. It felt as though an enormous weight had been lifted from his chest.

Oh, thank God, he said once more as he went past the lavatory door.

He was sitting there waiting for her to wake. Looked at her face, thin and bloodless, but calm now, quite calm in sleep. The small, dear face with the familiar features. . . .

A long, long time. Just sat there looking at her. . . .

At last her mouth began to twitch, it was distorted by pain—she opened her eyes. Bewildered—as though she didn't understand—what had happened to her?

Then she seemed to recollect—remembered. . . . The pain gave way to a wan, wan smile—happy. . . . She groped for his hand—raised herself a little.

"Where is it?"

She looked around the room.

"Where is it? Halvdan?"

He looked at her.

"Halvdan? Isn't it? Isn't it here? Halvdan!"

He stroked her head.

"They had to—had to think of you—sweetheart. . . ."

"Of me?"

She stared into him. "Of me? *Me!*"

"You mustn't—mustn't move—must lie still. . . ."

"Where is it?"

"You have hovered between life and death, darling Arna—you don't know—between life and death. . . ."

"Where is my child?"

He tried to press her down in the bed, but she propped herself up with her arms, had strength.

"They had to save you—darling. . . ."

She stared at him. Her eyes were like great holes.

"What have you done with my child?" she cried.

"Arna—darling Arna—you mustn't . . ."

"Where is it? I want to see it!"

He caressed her, shook his head.

"I want to see my child!"

"No, no—you must understand—it's impossible—*impossible*. . . ."

"What have you done with my child? What have you done?"

"Listen—Arna—it was necessary—they had to save you—sweetheart. . . ."

"Why should I be saved? What have you done with my child? What have you done with my child?" she screamed, flinging herself violently to and fro in the bed with a howl like an animal's. He had to hold her, call for the nurse.

They came running. The bandages were red. She had brought on a haemorrhage and had to be taken in hand.

The years passed. They lived very much to themselves, even more so than before, almost isolated. She didn't want to mix with people, would hardly meet anyone. And neither of them had any real need of it, at least not of social life and going out. He did not want it, either; didn't miss it. They kept to their home. Gave all their thoughts to it, to their home life, as it suited them best.

They didn't go abroad any more, didn't want to now. They were unlikely to have felt really happy anywhere else now. It was best for them here. And Arna wanted to be able to visit the grave. It was natural that she didn't want to be separated from that.

She lived in the memory of her child. It was something that filled her always, he noticed, though he didn't often care to touch on the subject. Something she couldn't get away from. All the things she had made for the baby were hidden. Where she kept them he didn't know, but they were still there. One evening when he had come back earlier than expected, he had found her with them in front of her on the table. And long afterward the same thing happened again when the performance at the theatre he was going to was cancelled. They made no mention of it on this occasion but went in and had a cup of tea, which he saw had been laid for her in the adjoining room, though she had forgotten about it. And then she played their favourite music for him in the gentle, intimate way she had if he asked her. He knew no one else who could play it in that way.

Even the little cot was still up in the attic, with bed-clothes, quilt and all. He had an idea that if it had not been for him she would have had it down in the flat. Perhaps she would. Would have had it about somewhere here.

In fact, she lived in her dreams of the child which had come into the world dead. Imagined how it was, would have been. What its personality would have been like, its little soul. And what it would have become, how it would have got on in life. After all, it was a human being like the rest of us, just as much as ourselves. Was a whole life, which had just never come alive. But which had existed all the same, just had never really been allowed to become what it should. But which she now experienced instead.

She was often out by the grave. And went there even more often than he knew of, somethimes when she was only out in town on an errand and came home somewhat later than he had expected. Tended the little mound, saw that the flowers were always quite fresh. And sat there on the seat engrossed in her thoughts. She would also go occasionally to her mother's grave, but more seldom; it was not in the same cemetery.

She seemed to think she owed a duty to this uncom-pleted life. But she also believed that the child existed. She was sure of it. Otherwise she could not have felt as she did, live together with it like that.

"What do you think about life after death?" she asked Halvdan once.

"We know so little about it, Arna."

"Yes. But perhaps it's our fault that we do know so little."

"Oh. . . . How do you mean?"

"Oh, perhaps it is."

He did not feel the same emptiness as she because they had no child. Only at the beginning really. He thought that they had each other after all.

They still had their love. Perhaps not in the same way as before, perhaps altered. But it was still there for them, inside them. It didn't seem to mean the same to her any more, not so much, that was plain. But it could be seen that it was there. She often said when they chanced to speak of it that she merely thought their feelings for one another had deepened. They had loved in another way before, more superficially or however you liked to put it. They had been too much taken up by the purely physical side of love, which is not Love itself and which cannot have such worth as one thinks, cannot give the *deepest* significance to two people's life together.

She seemed slightly aloof from this side of their love for each other, that which he thought had united them in such a beautiful way and made them so happy. And she felt far too dejected, as it were, to let herself go properly. When he was drawn to her she often repulsed him with a tired and pained expression. It was as if she wanted to say that she was of no use.

She appeared without desire. Seemed to have no actual need of him any longer. Lived within herself.

She wondered sometimes whom the child would have resembled. What it would have looked like. She didn't for a moment think it would have been like her, had anything of her. It would have been like *him*. And it had been a boy, too. It would have had *his* eyes and mouth and perhaps his way altogether, that affectionate way he had. And perhaps it would have been like him in other ways too, in spiritual qualities of deeper significance.

But it had never been allowed to live. She had not been able to bring his child into the world.

If only she had been able to see it just once and retain a memory of it. If she had been able to bring a living being into the world. But what she had borne had been dead. And had been *forced* to die. It had wanted to come alive, but had been forced. They had taken the child's life away from it, just taken everything from it for *her* sake. It had at once been made to die for its mother, for her. She who had already lived, who actually was not needed any more. Merely to save her. So it was compelled to sacrifice itself. And that put her under a special obligation to it; she had a secret debt which could never really be paid.

She tried to pay it as well as she could by at least being with the child as much as possible in her thoughts. And by trying to uplift herself, become a more worthwhile person than before, more tuned to the spiritual, to that which lies beyond what usually preoccupies us. By trying to live in the world where she knew her child was. The purely sensual must not mean so much to her any more, engross her so entirely.

It didn't, either. All this side of life, in fact, inspired her mostly with feelings of aversion nowadays. She felt it as something imperfect, in a way low, which dragged her down. And it really meant so little to her. She had overcome this in herself.

She had done this gradually. For even earlier it had begun to mean less and less to her, as she had become more aware of the way she was made, perhaps had also matured a little, if one could call it that. She had not become utterly indifferent to it. But still. . . . One longs nevertheless for something — hard to say what — for something else. Something which can satisfy the deepest, the innermost part of us, and which can impart renewal, cause something new to sprout within us. But it must come in another way, from another source.

This was what the child could have given her. If it had been granted to her to become a mother, to press the little one to her heart, have him at her breast. Put her arms around a small being who was *hers*, just hers. This, she felt, would have been the great new wonder. It would have made her a person of higher worth. Would have raised her out of her previous life, up to another and higher one.

But now it seemed for all that as though the child were trying to enter into her existence. As though this little being whom she had only hurt, only harmed, still wished her well. Still called to her, let her understand that it was there and could be reached by her tenderness, all her thoughts. As if it wanted her to know a mother's happiness after all. A supermundane joy, the soul's calm, incomprehensible happiness—if only she could raise herself to the world above us. It was as though it wanted to turn her mind and thoughts toward that world. Try to make her understand that we belong to it in spite of all.

As if it wanted to give her all that she had had to forgo, give it to her none the less. From the other side.

If only she could accept it. She felt so imperfect and unworthy. But she was changed all the same, she noticed that. Her eyes were turned more to the higher, essential things than before. And she knew now that there was a world other than this. A world where we really can meet. Where she could meet, be united with her child. And where she and Halvdan also could meet, find each other far more wholly and completely.

When he worried her by wanting to possess her, by his caresses, she would reproach him for not caring for her soul, her inner self. He would answer that of course he did. And it was true, in one way. But he still didn't do so in the way she longed for deep inside—that they should become part of each other. In the way they *could*.

And yet—they had so very much that united them. Common interests and sympathies. The whole of their mental make-up harmonized so well. They lived together quite happily, were nevertheless *one*. And Halvdan had this goodness and understanding which enclosed their life with a warmth of a purely inner, spiritual kind. She had never really deserved this constant goodness of his. The little she had been capable of doing for him, meaning to him, and the way she had failed him by not being able to bring his child into the world. . . . In reality it was she who was not worthy of *him*. But she was a little more so now at least than before.

He grew more and more reserved. Often seemed depressed. But then they had nothing to rejoice at after that happened, nothing to hope for any more. Their life was at an end in one way; it had never become just as they once dreamed it would. And the house felt empty when the little guest they expected had not come, never would come. Nothing was the same after this. It could be seen that they both felt it.

She often urged Halvdan to go out a little more. She thought he should if he wanted to; it did him good. And he had begun doing so of recent years. He went quite often to the theatre, and especially to concerts. To these he could also coax her once in a while, if it was something really worth hearing. But otherwise she never went with him, never to a restaurant or in fact anywhere. He had to go with an acquaintance or—more often than not—alone.

That kind of thing seemed to give her no pleasure and she never liked being with a lot of people. Whatever the reason was. Perhaps she felt sensitive about her limp, thought it was noticeable.

He did find a certain diversion in these brief outings, even if his home was the only place he really needed and where he preferred to spend his time, But he didn't make her happy by staying at home, either.

He couldn't really quite make her out any longer. She

was so unlike herself in many ways, had become so. It was not the same any more.

Naturally he thought it was going too far, this business with the child. And yet at the same time he felt sorry for her that she took it in that way. That she really *suffered* from it so much. But that was no reason why it should affect the whole of their life together, almost separate them and cast a gloom over everything like this.

After all, it was not something which meant *everything* to them. They still had much to make them happy, to live for, if they would make the most of it. They had each other. Their love, their feelings for one another—they still had those.

True, the erotic side was no longer the same for him, either. He could not feel like that for her any more. But she was the woman he loved and with whom he wanted to live after all. Nothing had altered in regard to that.

When she kept on with those reproaches that he did not love her soul, cared nothing for it, he could not help at last saying that surely he had always done so. It must be obvious to anyone, and otherwise there could never have been anything between them.

He couldn't see why she wanted to make such utterly pointless statements. And, after all, it was so *unjust*.

He had devoted himself to her as completely as it was ever possible to imagine. Worshipped her, in fact. Lived his life, all these years, only for her, for this woman who meant everything to him. Why, he had been so filled by his love that all this time he had hardly ever had a thought that it was a lame woman he loved. He hadn't bothered his head about it, scarcely been aware of it even. Those, actually, were the feelings he had for her.

It was really her *inner self* that he loved. Not first and foremost her body, but her *inner self*. Therein lay the secret of his love, he well knew that.

He couldn't quite explain, but she had something oddly

subduing, something which drew him to her—he didn't
know what. And she still had it.

It had the effect of making him overlook her deformity.
He almost thought it suited her, was part of her. Was part
of her personality to be like that.

She won him and kept him purely and simply by her
inner self, by attracting him in some way. There was something restrained, unexpressed about her, something which
seemed to give a secret excitement.

Something. He couldn't say what.

And yet. Perhaps it was very largely her deformity and
nothing else which had made her as she was. Which had
given her this indescribable something.

It was very likely. That it had meant a lot to the shaping
of her being, her personality, however strange the thought
might be. Which had given her this fragile and taut
quality, and also probably the introversion which she had,
which she had always had.

Yes. It was no doubt very largely her deformity which
had made her just as she was.

Now she had changed in several respects, both outwardly and inwardly. The face's peculiar beauty was still
there, but the years of course had left their mark, and her
appearance showed this; there was a sharpness about the
features. The eyes were most like themselves. They were
still beautiful and fascinating in their eloquence. But the
expression in them was now highly strung and nervous—
as she was herself, must be, for everything pointed to it.

On the whole there was now something about her which
made him feel sorry for her.

And she did nothing to keep herself up, pull herself
together; to stand her ground. She merely gave way to her
sad moods and made herself, without knowing it, a burden
to those around her. One felt so dejected in her presence,
there was no getting away from it.

She evidently gave no thought to it, or to the effect she

had in general. It seemed as though she was indifferent to all such matters. Nor was she any longer so interested in dress, though she didn't actually neglect it. And when she walked the limp was more apparent; she no longer seemed to bother to conceal it. Previously it had almost had the effect of something interesting about her which gave a painful and fragile quality to her beauty, almost suited it, and she had also had a gliding walk which made it scarcely noticeable. But with the years, and when she gave little heed to it, it was apparent in a different way; one's attention was drawn to it. She became more of a woman who was lame.

And yet, he loved her just as much. He couldn't doubt it. He longed for her—for what she had been, for their former life together. For their love, all his tenderness to her; would like to have shown it to her again. That is how he felt for her. It hurt him to see her tired face with its suffering expression, in which he sought, more and more in vain, the image which had been and still was so dear to him.

It could not be helped; somehow a kind of oppression came over them both and over their life together at home. They went their own ways, as it were, he often in a mood of irritation, which, however, she always bore with submissive equanimity.

She was worried by not really knowing what he thought about the soul's life after death—what his religious views were. She for her part had gradually come to believe, really believe. Without prejudices, without any dogmas, but nevertheless had attained a definite belief that there is something over and beyond what we see and conceive. In one way he shared this, was familiar with her thoughts; occasionally they could talk about it all. But she didn't know if he really *believed*. And it tormented her not to know anything definite about it. For she wanted to have *everything* in common with him, especially something so vital, the most important thing there was. If he did not share it with her she did not feel it had the same worth. Nor the same security. It was not a real faith. Only *they* could feel security. They together.

When he got outside the house he felt relieved, and that was really the only reason why he went out. He took no particular pleasure in it otherwise. But he liked to sit in a café of an evening to read the newspapers, or just to have somewhere to sit, perhaps see a few people. He could not help noticing, either, that there were other women and it struck him sometimes how odd it was that he lived, and would no doubt live all his life, together with one whom fundamentally perhaps he had not so much in common with after all, perhaps not as he had thought. And that it was a lame woman to whom he had become attached in this way for always—was to share his life with. But it was she whom he loved. That was the reason for it all, as is so often the way.

One thing had occurred to him recently. He wondered whether the big change in her might not be due to ill health. She did not look well. But perhaps she never had, for that matter. It was more apparent now, however, he thought; he could tell from her complexion, which had taken on a greyish, unhealthy look. And from so many other things, too. Something was certainly wrong. So it seemed, anyway.

She asked one evening if he thought she should go to the doctor, because she didn't feel quite up to the mark, and she hardly ever got any proper sleep. It was mostly because of that. It was hard always to lie awake so much at night.

He looked up, over at her. Went and sat beside her.

Of course she should. Of course she must go! They would go together the very next day. He questioned her, how she felt, if she had pain anywhere—oh no, none at all. But her heart?

"It's probably your heart, Arna dear."

"Oh, there's nothing much wrong with that."

But he thought so anyway. How long had she felt like this?

"Oh, I can't really say. Quite a long time, I suppose."

He looked at her—into her frank, tired eyes, which had sunk far in. Held her head between his hands.

They went to the doctor next day.

No, her heart was not good. But he also suspected something else, that she might be suffering from some blood disease; there was quite a lot that pointed to it. And her resistance was particularly low. A test was taken which would be examined.

They strolled home through the streets. Held each other's hand right in the middle of town.

It appeared that she was suffering from pernicious anaemia. Had little more than a fifth of the red corpuscles she should have. It was at the stage when she had perhaps had the disease for several years.

He was quite broken when they were told. But she seemed calm. And she didn't appear especially depressed. It will be all right, was all she said.

It was not essential for her to go to bed. But she was to keep to a certain diet. And she was to have arsenic.

When he went about anxiously, his face slack, utterly transformed, she drew him to her and stroked his cheek. "What is it, darling? My own dear one." Smiled her tranquil smile at him.

She didn't seem to understand what it was all about.

He hinted that it was something serious.

"Oh, it's nothing to worry about," she said.

"But Arna dear, don't you see—it's very serious. It's a disease which can lead to—perhaps to death."

"Yes. But I am not afraid of death, Halvdan."

He threw himself down beside her and seized her arms. Did she want to leave him then? Were they to part, *they*, the two of them—from each other? . . .

"No, Halvdan, we shall not part. You don't believe that, Halvdan."

They talked for a long time. She explained the way she believed it was and how little death meant. It could not part them when they belonged so much together. It wasn't like that at all. He put his head in her lap and cried—could not hold back the tears. Looked at her, into her perfectly calm face with its pallor spiritualized by suffering. There were no tears in her eyes, they merely shone. And she nodded to him as she did when there was something special, in that thoughtful way which he recognized so well. Took him to her and kissed him.

They returned again to this whenever they talked together. Wanted to talk so—about it. And they talked often, often. Lived in each other, in each other's open, wide open soul which kept watch day after day, unceasingly. It was like a perpetual festival, intimate and tremblingly big.

She wanted him to come to her. Yes. She longed for him, for him, her beloved; stretched herself after him—as she would do always, always.

It was something they had never before felt, this infinite, calm tendernes, this love quite without desire, only a complete mergence in each other. Was something incomprehensible — pain and happiness, and a reverence which raised it above everything, made it a wonder of which they could only divine a part, a rite in a mystery. However they had loved one another—this they had never felt, not this reverence which can fill one only in the immediate vicinity of death, when one is to be wrenched out of the loved one's arms.

They could lie afterward and stare with burning eyes into the darkness of the room, in mute melancholy, holding each other's hand. Until perhaps she might fall asleep for a while and he heard her breathe quietly. Lay listening. He didn't want to fall asleep before she did. Ever to sleep more than she.

In the daytime they were never apart from each other now. Their life was one, it moved along day by day and week by week toward that which awaited them.

They spoke of all that had been. Of all they had done together, shared so completely with each other.

"Yes, we have been happy, Halvdan. Happy as few people have been," she said, stroking his head with her thin little hand which no longer seemed to have any weight. "We have always had everything in common. From the time we first met, Halvdan."

"That time. Do you remember?"

Yes. They had not met as so many others, as is usual with two young people. Not like that. It had never been like that for them.

And all they had felt and seen, all they had experienced together since—always had everything together.

Yes, they remembered. Remembered so much during this time. And they could, now that they looked back, feel their life as something so full and rich—it had become that through their great love. Acquired its deep meaning from it, from this intimate unity in all things.

She said once that they had no right to complain, for no life could be more lovely than theirs. None more complete in its happiness. They must give thanks for what had been given them. Give thanks—and be prepared to pay back their loan of earthly happiness.

But that within them which had made it possible for them to feel all this, that would be saved from death, could never perish. It was too great and precious to perish.

They lived in something so enclosed, so by itself, that it was as if only they two existed. And in a pure air in which pain seemed easy to bear, even death itself. Her calm trust could not help affecting him, making him feel as he never thought he could do in the face of death. Gave him peace in the midst of suffering, so that it could not break him down utterly.

The child slipped more into the background; not even she spoke much about it any longer. They were the ones concerned now. Their souls, which would not be parted; which belonged together for ever. They both believed that. It was that which kept them up, made them so strong and full of reliance. Of the brightest hope.

She was his bride who was leaving on a journey. And then they would meet again. Yes, soon again. The two of them.

This was no longer love. It must be called by some other name, even greater and more sacred. And as she lay pale and wasted in her bed her gaze shone with the light from the world which she already seemed to discern, to have already become so familiar with.

She had been bedridden now for a long time. Her strength was used up; she had not had much in reserve. Only her soul retained its power. The body awaited its disintegration, wanted it. She was tormented almost constantly by a severe headache. And the little she was able to eat she often could not keep down. But it seemed as though she no longer needed nourishment in order to exist. She might live for a time yet—none could say how long. But with her weak heart the flame of life could be blown out at any moment.

He sat continually by her side. Practically never left her.

And they could talk. She could converse just as clearly as before. In the stillness which prevailed around them, which prevails when death is expected, they spoke of what was to come. Promised to live in each other, which we can even after death—to overcome it.

Yes, yes. She would always be with him. He would always feel her presence.

She made him promise that he would be quite calm and still at her death. That's how it should be. That was the right, the only right way. And he said that he would try, in spite of everything, because she had asked him.

They could speak of such things without becoming upset, without pain as it were. They could now, they had attained that—attained such peace. . . .

No—there is no such boundary between life and death, not as one thinks. Like a ship putting out to sea, which is to sail far, far away—we see it sink on the horizon, as into the depths, for ever, into an endless distance. . . .

But he who lies lost in gentle melancholy on the shore can see it disappear behind a flower.

One evening as he sat holding her hand in the dusk he felt that it had grown colder. Bending over her he saw that she was dead. That she had left him. . . .

He didn't cry. No, he didn't cry. Only looked, looked at her—remained sitting with her hand in his—with his beloved's hand in his—as before—quite as before. . . .

No, no, there was no parting—no boundary. . . .

No boundary—Nothing had happened. . . .

Only closed her eyes—closed them—lightly—until they should shine at him in another world.

Not until later, after the funeral and all that had to be, did he really understand what had happened, feel all the frightful emptiness after her. Feel that he had been left *alone*. Utterly alone.

Moved about the flat, to and fro in the rooms, with the servants who kept it tidy as before and cooked his food, which he hardly touched. Everything was as before. Exactly as they had had it, as he was used to. Everything reminded him that she had left him.

The corner of the sofa where she used to sit, the table in the living-room where they used to have their tea, with the chair opposite. . . . And each thing in the whole house, in her room, in all the rooms—everything was there just as before. Everything reminded him that she had left it.

On the grand piano was her music. And on the stand a

piece stood open at the page she had been playing the last evening she was up. He tried it himself once, but he played so badly, it didn't sound the same as when she played. So it would never be played any more. Looked into her room—there was no one there. Could feel so well that there was no one in that room. Lifted the flap and glanced into her sewing-table with its cotton reels and skeins of wool. And the dressing-table with the powder box, the cut-glass flasks, and the silver hand-mirror which had so often reflected her image and now only his own. It was only he. No one but he in the whole house.

And by the window in the living-room her armchair, where she had liked to sit of late. The cushion which she used to have at her back. . . .

It was a constant torture he endured. It was there every morning when he got up, to be gone through again. Over and over again. Each day was a torment to him, a burden which he could hardly bear or had the strength for any more. He went to pieces, looked wasted and wretched, completely changed. Only a shadow of what he had been. He scarcely recognized himself.

And this awful emptiness, emptiness. . . .

Six months went by, a year.

At last it was plain to him that he couldn't go on like this. He couldn't stand it among all the memories; he must not live for *them*. Not torture himself with them, everlastingly. He was to live in *her*, in her soul.

No, this was not what she had wanted, and which he had promised. She wanted his sorrow to be calm and controlled. A bright and tranquil sorrow, full of hope and trust. They would see each other again. Were to meet again.

He must try to get away from this sombre despair which only oppressed him. It was his duty to try.

But he didn't know what to do with himself. Where he should go. It was so utterly immaterial to him. But he must do something to get away, just get away somewhere.

So he gave the servants notice. And the home was to be broken up. He was going to travel—didn't know how long he would be away, perhaps for a long time. Everything was to be packed up and stored.

Even up to the last he was not quite clear where he was going. Finally he decided on Paris, so as to have it settled. He couldn't face solitude, the seclusion in the country which he loved most. He needed people around him as he was now.

Arriving down there, he put up at a simple hotel which fell short of his requirements, but he didn't want anything else. Walked about in the crowd. Heard the wailing of the cars, the buses thundering against the road surface, the trams clanging incessantly among the throngs between the pavements. And the newsvendors' hoarse shouts through the autumn mist. Why was he here?

He went about abstractedly, aloof and alien to what went on around him. It was incapable of engaging him, diverting him in any way. He felt even more lonely in this swarm of people, in the rush and bustle. Still thought of nothing but her, only wanted to think of, live in her. He made a pilgrimage to one or two places which they had visited together. Walked along streets where they had walked. And down by the Seine, on the side where he remembered they had walked one lovely spring day the first time they were in Paris. Sought out a restaurant where they used to eat then. And otherwise just drifted about, aimlessly, between the dirty rows of houses, shut in by the wet mist which never lifted. Without any real goal once he had relived this past.

The air was sticky, as in a brewery. Sometimes it hung in the streets all day, yellow as sulphur. The asphalt was slippery with dirt and moisture. One seemed to go down into something subterranean, into an unreal world down underneath something, full of an undefined life. Until,

toward evening, the lights came on, the headlights from
cars began to sweep over the asphalt, the advertisements
glowed and flickered, twisting up the façades, everything
grew hectic, feverish in the fog, as if fermenting. People
altered, their faces were tense, lively, they jostled in front
of the lighted entrances. The women began to prowl the
streets and whisper to passers-by. Someone laughed there
in front, and somewhere behind the limousines glided past
with women in evening dress and swelling furs, like large
animals. The cafés lay in dazzling light, full of people, a
constant stream in and out. The whole boulevard seethed
with life under the naked trees, stank of powder and
gasoline.

He turned into the side streets where it was badly lighted
and he could go in peace. Far away from the main streets,
just walked. His thoughts with her, his hot, burdensome
thoughts. Took out her little mother-of-pearl penknife
which he always carried, put it in his coat pocket so that he
could feel it. He thought she was near him, that he could
feel her. Perhaps she was here with him.

At last he had walked so far that he didn't quite know
where he was, had to go down into the Metro to get home.
Stood in the crowded train, all the seats were taken. Tired,
pallid faces. Held on to the strap, gazing straight ahead of
him like the others, out into the tunnel, at the dripping wall
with the small lamps. He had gone grey at the temples,
though otherwise he showed no particular signs of age.
Jostled with the others through the barrier and up the steps
in the muggy air. Went back to his hotel.

Winter had set in with its almost ceaseless rain. But one
got used to the rain; it seemed part of it all. And it didn't
matter to him. On the contrary it suited him, these trick-
ling wet days. He didn't want any light, any joy. Wanted
to be cooped up. In this quiet greyness, and with the even,
rather far-off restlessness around him. He no longer wished
for any pleasure from existence, nor could he have it. He

must go on living. But that was all. Went about like a recluse, without mixing with anyone. Hidden away as one can be in a big city, stuck in among the others.

He could be quite alone with his thoughts—and that was a great comfort. Alone with his sorrow. With what he wanted. Could live in his world, didn't matter which.

And the flurry, the nervous rushing about gave a kind of calm to the senses. Mostly, perhaps, because he didn't take part in this life. Stood so detached from everything. Then it gave a kind of hollow peace.

He could immerse himself entirely in the past, as he wished.

Often in the evenings he would stroll down by the Seine, away past Nôtre Dame, in the half light and partial stillness which lay over the quay here, and see the station clock gleam at the *gare* in the distance. It made him think of her. Of how she was resting there away up in the north—the cold, frozen earth. Consigned to it—and so far, so infinitely far away from him—perhaps snow on the grave. White, virgin snow.

She whom he had loved, she who had been *his*. . . .

And now hidden down in the earth. Forsaken—but always, always living in his burning thoughts.

Yes, he was with her, constantly. His love burned as always, as it had done all along, only with a clearer and purer flame now. It had become something higher, something completely spiritualized, freed from everything mundane.

Yes. He thought of his love. . . . The whole of his life stood out before him—how strange it had been, had turned out. So filled with a single great feeling. So dedicated to *one thing*. To her.

The feeling she had inspired in him had determined his destiny. And still did, would do so until his death. He gave everything to love, full and undivided. And became happy by it, happy even in the midst of his sorrow, his bitter loss.

It was the altar to which he had once been led as though
by an invisible hand and to which he had remained faith-
ful. He would be found on the step up to it when he could
go on no longer down here, still kneeling in death.

Such was his fate—that which had given him his life.
Something completed now, already past, now that she had
died. But in which he still lived. Which lifted his soul above
this continued existence without aim and meaning, watching over him and helping him to endure.

He could go as in an ecstasy during these solitary walks.
Feel a sublimity and emotion which took his mind away
from the present, to a higher world. And when he turned
homeward through narrow streets, his raised eyes could see
the sky flaming red between the murky houses. The night
sky of the metropolis—and yet not it. It was like a vision,
an opened, bleeding space he saw.

So this long, heavy winter passed—the longest he could
ever remember, though in reality not so—a short time
compared with that at home. And there was a sense of
spring. The rawness in the air was offset by swift gusts, felt
like warm, light breaths when he turned a corner. The
atmosphere changed, the clouds parted and scudded on,
were driven together again. At night it rained. And in a
few days everything was transformed, quite a different
mildness than before, a moist, drifting warmth. The coming
spring.

But this time which had passed had told on him, had
clearly left its mark. His face was sunken and grey, and his
eyes had grown hot and restless. He had a dull, worn air.
Tired, decrepit.

He didn't want any spring. Didn't want it to be so
beautiful again. He knew that it would only make every-
ing so much harder. Sensed a painful, inner unease at the
light, the reawakening. But he couldn't help feeling relieved
in this new air, that he could breathe again. Sat in the sun
in the little Cluny gardens or in the Luxembourg, which

was full of scents and the twitter of birds. The trees burst into leaf, violently; each day there was a difference. Out in the boulevards it gleamed, too. A light, green haze everywhere. As in a hothouse, suddenly, everything burst out in the moist warmth. After rain it felt as though it steamed from the warm asphalt.

The whole city took on a light and soft air, a pale shimmer, one could now see so far. Away across to distant parts of the city which faded out in the thin sunlight. And the parks which were turning green far away on the other side of the Seine. It was like walking about in quite a new city.

People everywhere out for a stroll. And the cafés were empty; everyone sat outside in the sun, squashed together at the tables. Chatter and the hum of voices. He drifted along the street under the light, sparse trees which had no shadow.

Found himself a seat outside a bar where there were not so many people. Sat and watched the life. The passers-by. His collar was not quite clean, nor was the shirt down by the cuffs. He had begun to neglect such things, without knowing it.

And toward evening. The mild air. The long, enervating sweetness which seemed to ebb out in the very atmosphere, in the pale opal of the sky. The lights were put on outside the cafés even before it was dark and mixed with the daylight. Women sat at the tables sipping a drink with their legs out in the street.

As the weather got warmer the evenings were the most pleasant and one had to walk and walk in this tepid, saturated spring. Couldn't remain sitting inside. The very air had something attractive which invited an endless roving without a goal. When darkness fell, the boulevards streamed with light and the greenery shone transparent around the lamps. In front of the innumerable pavement cafés the foliage was illuminated as at nocturnal pastorales.

He sat down at a table after the long, hot day. The heat had already set in and the days felt almost oppressive. This spring in the heart of the city was curiously enervating. But he felt an inner tiredness, too; perhaps that was why. And that was perhaps due to his walking so much. Almost constantly. As if he must always keep walking.

A woman was sitting at a table near him. Rather fat, with long bare arms under her silk cape. Powdered white and painted, with a cigarette between the protruding red lips. Was drinking something with grenadine, sucking it up in a straw.

There was music inside; some music-hall songs were being played for empty walls and a solitary couple over in a corner.

She tapped the ash off her cigarette, took a few whiffs and dropped it on to her plate. Gave him a quick glance and tucked her hair into her hat. Crossed her legs. Rubbed her palms together slowly, her face averted and her thoughts far away. The nails were pink and brightly polished, had large white moons. Got out another cigarette and lighted it, the cape slid off on one side and her arm was bared up to the shoulder. The nipple stuck out.

Another one came up from the pavement, sat down beside her and took out her powder.

He had emptied his glass and he set off into the crowd.

Walked again. As before. Although he was really too tired. Walked and walked.

It was almost sultry. Warm and no breeze, not the coolness toward night which there usually was.

The boulevards shone, crossed each other and stretched out in all directions. The city had burst out like a flower, too large and full of its confined scent to close. It was almost stupefying. He walked in a kind of trance.

Dense with people. Couples which drifted along the pavements, leaning against each other. By the shrubbery prowling women with their everlasting "*cheri*." The noise

out in the road was muffled, had an unfamiliar sound.
Life dozed, stationary.

He felt such exhaustion that he could hardly go on.
Went into a bar and sat down at a table which was just
vacant. Drank something strong with a lot of gin in it, two
or three drinks one after the other in order to numb himself. Inside was some kind of luxury place with dancing,
half full of people and with champagne on the tables. The
blare of saxophones and the rattle of banjos could be heard
when the velvet curtain was drawn aside for elegant couples
to go in.

One or two demimondaines sat perched up on the high
stools at the bar. Looked at him in the mirror and blew the
smoke out in a thin stream with pouted lips. They were
talking to the bartender and drinking something cheap.
Sat on the edge of the stools with their thighs crossed. After
a while they were joined by some young men. One of the
girls pulled off her hat and shook out her hair, shouting for
three Manhattans. They started to get drunk.

In there behind the curtain the music thumped.
Streamers swam in the air, he could see, when the waiter
drew aside the curtain. He went in.

There was a soft carpet which he sank deep down into.
Bare in the middle and crowded with dancers. The room
was now crammed with people. Laughter and noise, full
of balloons and bellowing from cardboard trumpets.
Everyone shouted. The music thumped against the walls.
It was so hot that he sweated.

He danced once or twice. Drank bad champagne. She
had long eyelashes and a little vanity case at her knee.
Thin, quivering nostrils like those of a newly captured
animal. Her gums were bright red like fish's gills when
she laughed. She laughed in some way the whole time.

The heat here was appalling. The air was thick. The

streamers did not sink, they writhed through the smoke, the room seemed full of wriggling worms. A woman started crying at the next table with her eyes staring and lustrous; they nudged her to make her stop. The Negro orchestra twitched and jumped in their chairs; the sweat ran down inside their collars. Out among the dancers glided a slim, blonde woman with a blue birthmark on her back and shaved in the armpits. Twisted in time to the tango, pressed her thigh in between her partner's legs.

He had drunk more than he was used to. But the champagne felt slightly cooling after the short drinks. He got up and left.

Drifted about the streets. Just drifted and drifted, for hours on end. Didn't know where he was or where he had been. But that he had been sitting on a seat somewhere for a long time. Had come to because he felt cold.

The early morning chill made itself felt. But it was still quite dark. Fat rats ran across the pavement, down into the grating around the trees. The latrine carts rattled through the empty streets. Down in a basement opening there was a light, there was the smell of new-baked bread. He stopped and drew in his breath, stood looking absently down at a man who was busy at the oven.

One or two places opened up. Dirty sawdust with cigarette butts and matches was swept out. He stepped inside and up to a counter to get a cup of coffee and a fresh brioche. Taxi-drivers and workmen in leather jackets were sitting at the long tables and at the counter were some loafers with cigarettes stuck fast to their lips. A jaded woman accosted him; the nipples on her breasts stuck out. She spoke hoarsely, with a voice like a man's. Her gums were liver-brown when she smiled; she looked tarnished in some way.

As he went on home it started to get light. A slender little woman with her coat drawn tightly around her was walking in front; her bottom waggled at each step. The

Metro had just reopened and the musty vapours rose up like a feverish breath. Pale people came up out of the earth, hurried away. Clattered against the paving-stones.

He hardly had the strength left to stand upright. Walked in a deep, dull stupor. His lacklustre eyes had a staring look. Quite empty, as though burned out. He had become like someone else. Or something else. Something besides himself.

He dragged himself home.

Some days afterwards he sat writing a long letter. He appeared quite calm. His eyes had regained their former brightness. Perhaps a greater brightness than before, deeper. There was something quiet and beautiful about him as he sat in the simply furnished room collecting his thoughts, finishing his letters.

Dear Brother:

I am writing this for a special reason, which I shall try to explain to you as well as I can in the following. As my brother you are the one to whom I wish to, and should, turn, and I think I can do so in the hope of being understood. Apart from you, I have no one now. No one in any way close to me.

Since I came down here you have not heard much from me, but that's because I've had nothing to tell you other than what you already know, that I am living here in my sorrow, in my extreme distress at the loss which has afflicted me. You know what my beloved wife meant to me. Yet not, perhaps, that she meant *everything*. That when she was taken from me I had nothing left, nothing to live for—*nothing*. That she was my life.

We two had everything in common. Every thought, every wish—joy and sorrow, everything. And every day from the time we met until the evening when she went away from here, leaving me in this terrifying loneliness. I know nothing of love apart from what I myself have felt, but it seems to me that it is not possible for the human heart to experience it more deeply, more wholly and completely. From my knowledge of it, it stands out for me as something sacred, something so sublime and immeasurably great. It seems like one great mystery in which I have been allowed to share. And all this *she* has given me. It is bound up with her pure figure, with the memory of what she was to me, she who is no longer with me.

As I sit here tonight looking back, it seems as if she has given my existence its meaning, as if she has lifted it up from nothing and filled it with the most beautiful and costly things which life can give us. I don't know if you understand me when I speak of love in this way; if you believe that it can mean so infinitely much. But that's how it is for *me*. Your life has been so different in all respects. You have devoted yourself to your work, been taken up by so many different things. While I have lived only for *one*. For this one thing alone. Apart from that I have had nothing and have been unable to come to grips with anything properly. And it is this which you find hard to understand perhaps, and which for *you* perhaps appears as a fault. But my life has been full. Wonderfully full. I'm not setting it up against my fellow man's, still less do I want to vaunt it in any way. I merely say that that's how I feel it. And what more can we know? What else have we to go by than the fullness of our heart when we look back.

After what I have now said you can perhaps form some idea of my loss and pain. Of how utterly desolate and empty this world must be for me now that *she* has left it and I am only a stranger here. In fact, I no longer have any life. No real life other than

in the memory of her. In that I love and exist, only in
that. She shines for me in a glorified light to which I
reach out, at which I gaze in ardent longing, just as the
homeless man can stand for hours under the trees looking
into the glow from his lost home. Around me is darkness.
Only there is it light.

I hope you will understand; I beg you to. Understand
that I want to go where she is, that I want to move on
from here, where I own nothing, and go to meet her
where she is waiting for me. Yes, I know that she is
waiting for me. That she *exists*, that she is *alive*! Those
were our last words to each other, that death means so
little, that what happens is not real. And that it cannot
part us. I have sometimes felt, too, that she was near
me, sensed that she has been with me and watched over
me, even that she has gently stroked my forehead, as it
were, when I was desperate. . . . But now I want to go
where her soul has its glorious abode and where we shall
be wholly united, for always. Where nothing can ever
separate us again.

I beg you not to judge—to forgive—and not to
grieve over what has happened. There is no occasion
for sorrow, *none*. If you could see me as I sit here you
would say, this must be a happy man. And I *am* happy.
And that is why you must not pity me and not grieve. I
am going to celebrate the festival which awaits me.

I shall meet death with the same calm as she. And
I know that it will be so easy for me. For I am following
now the dictates of my heart, doing what it wants. That
is why I am so safe. I am merely fulfilling my destiny,
as it should be fulfilled. Whatever I have been like, I
have nevertheless loved her above all else in the whole
of my life. And to die for her sake is the only happiness
left to me. A great and tranquil happiness which she still
wants to give me.

I want to be taken home. And I will rest by her side.

I ask you to see to this, and I am sure that this wish of mine will be carried out, that you will do me this last favour.

I ask you also to have a stone erected on our grave, just a simple stone with our names. And beneath them an inscription, these words:

Life united them forever.

Farewell! And forgive me—and thank you for everything. . . .

You are the only one to whom I need say farewell. . . .

And I thank this life for what it gave—for her, for my love. . . . For all this which is not to perish. . . . No, which I know cannot perish.

Thank you for everything. . . . And farewell. . . .

Yours,

Halvdan

He folded the letter and wrote the address. Stood up. Took a deep breath. Felt such peace. Looked around the room. Went slowly down the stairs. There was no one about at this time. Only the concierge at the bottom who said his *Bon soir, monsieur,* and wondered why he was going out so late, after midnight.

The air was warm and a trifle sultry. He headed for a post box which he sometimes used. Dropped his letter in after holding it for a moment by the corner. And then wandered toward the Seine, to a part of the quay which was usually deserted at this time of night. Sat down on a seat which was in shadow.

When he had taken the dose he remained sitting quite still, his gaze turned to the somewhat misty sky—wanted to look *there*. His eyes shone with a deep and secret fire and he seemed to be smiling.

Felt the poison beginning to work, to deaden him, as he thought it would. Still heard the clocks strike—one, half-past one—as they measured out the time in a strange, far-off world. . . . Then he just went numb. His head sank a little to one side and he grew quite still. No longer existed.

A passing dog nosed his sock, lifted his leg and pee'd on him.

This was our visit to the land where the souls live. There it is not like here. They have an existence above this, a higher and more perfect one which shines toward us with its light. It is the soul's land, its real home. And in that land there is always festival. There it is always masquerade.

The Myth of Mankind

ONCE upon a time there was a world. Two people came to it one morning, but not to stay there for long, only for a short visit. They had many other worlds as well; this one seemed to them more insignificant and poorer than the others. It was beautiful here with the trees and the large drifting clouds, it was beautiful with the mountains, with the woods and glades, and with the wind which came, invisible, as it began to grow dark and touched everything so mysteriously; but it was nothing compared with the worlds they owned far away. That is why they wanted to stay only for a little while. But they did want to be there for a time, for they loved one another, and it was as if their love had nowhere been so wondrous as here. It seemed as though love was not something to be taken for granted in this world, something which completely filled everything, but that it was received as a guest of whom was expected the greatest things that could possibly happen here. It was, in fact, as if all that was clearest and brightest in their being became as secret here, as obscure, veiled, as if it were being kept hidden from them. They were strangers here, alone, left to the mercy of unknown powers. And the love that united them was a miracle, something that could be annihilated, that could wither away and die. That is why they wanted to stay only for a little while.

In this world it was not always day. After the light, dusk fell over everything; it was obliterated, was no longer there. They lay in the darkness, listening. They heard the wind soughing heavily in the trees. They crept together beneath them. "Why do we live here?"

The man made a house for them, only of moss and stones because they were soon to move on again. The woman spread fragrant grass on the trodden-down floor and waited for him when evening came. They loved one another more deeply than they ever seemed to have done before, and carried out the tasks of life here laid upon them.

One day as the man was roaming about in the woods he got such a longing for her whom he held dear above all else that he knelt down and kissed the earth because she had rested on it. But the woman began to love the clouds and the great trees, because the man returned home beneath them, and she loved the hour of twilight because it was then that he came. It was an unfamiliar world; it was not like those they owned far away.

And the woman bore a son. The holly trees outside the house sang for him; he looked wonderingly about him and then fell asleep to the sound, unafraid. But the man came home each evening with bleeding animals; he was tired and lay down heavily. They talked to each other happily in the darkness, they would soon be making a move now.

How strange it was, this world; after the summer came autumn and a cold winter, after the winter the most delightful spring. In this way they could see how time passed, everything here was changeable. The woman again bore a son, and after a few years yet another. The children grew up, they began to do things for themselves, running about and playing and finding something new every day. They just played with the whole strange world, with everything in it. What was meant in all seriousness they turned into something meant only for themselves. The man's hands grew rough from working with the soil and from his labours in the woods. The woman's features began to harden, too, and she walked more slowly, but her voice was gentle and singing as before.

One evening when she had settled down in the twilight, tired after a long day, with the children gathered around her, she said to them; "Now we shall soon be leaving here, now we shall soon be going away to the other worlds where we have our home."

The children looked at her in wonder. "What do you mean, Mother? Are there other worlds than this?"

Then she and the man looked at each other, a stab went through them, a smarting pain.

She answered in a lower voice, "Of course there are other worlds than this." And she began to tell them, tell them about these worlds that were so different from the one they lived in now; where everything was so much bigger and more wonderful than here, so light and happy, where there was not this darkness, where no trees soughed as they did here, where no struggle weighed down as this one did. The children closed around her, listening, now and then looking wonderingly over at the father as if to ask whether it was true. He nodded his head, lost in thought. The smallest sat right against the mother's feet; he was pale, his eyes gleamed with a strange light. But the eldest son, who was twelve years old, sat farther away, looking down at the ground; at last he got up and went out into the darkness.

The mother went on, they listened and listened; it was as if she were looking away into the distance, her gaze was far off; sometimes she fell silent, just as if she could not see, could not remember anything more, as if she had forgotten; then she spoke again, in a voice even more remote than before. The fire flickered on the sooty hearth, lighting up their faces, casting its glow around the heated room; the father held his hand before his face, the children listened with shining eyes. They sat like this, motionless, until it was almost midnight. Then the door opened, letting in the cold air from outside, and the eldest son came in. He looked around him. In his hand he had a large black bird with a grey belly. Blood ran from its breast; it was the first he had brought down himself. He threw it down on the ground

beside the fire. The warm blood steamed. Without a word
he went farthest into the semi-darkness and lay down to
sleep.

There was not a sound. The mother stopped speaking.
They looked wonderingly at the bleeding bird, which was
staining the ground red around its breast. They got up in
silence and all went to rest.

After that evening they didn't speak together very much
for a time, each going his own way. It was summer, the
bumblebees hummed, the grass round about was lush, the
glades were green after the spring rain that had fallen, the
air was so clear. One day the smallest boy went up to the
mother as she sat outside the house at noonday. He was pale
and quiet, and asked her to tell him about another world.
The mother looked up in surprise. "I can't talk to you
about this now, dear. The sun is high in the heavens; why
aren't you playing with all that is yours?" He left her
without a word and cried, unknown to anyone.

He never asked again. He just grew paler and paler, his
eyes burned with a strange lustre; one morning he had to
lie where he was, couldn't raise himself up. He lay motionless day after day, hardly speaking, just looking into the far
distance with his dilated eyes. They asked him if he was in
pain. They said that he would soon be able to go out into
the sun again, there were other flowers now, bigger than
before; he didn't answer, seemed not to see them. The
mother watched over him and cried; she asked if he would
like her to tell him all the wonderful things she knew, but
he smiled and just lay still as before.

And one evening he closed his eyes and was dead. They
all gathered around him. The mother laid his small hands
across his breast. Later, when the twilight came, they sat
together in the darkened room, speaking about him in
whispers. Now he had left this world. Now he was no
longer here. Now he had gone to another world, better and
happier than this one. But they said it despondently, sigh-

ing heavily. Shyly they went to rest on the far side from the dead boy; he lay lonely and cold.

In the morning they buried him in the earth; he was to lie there. The country smelled sweet, the sun shone everywhere, soft and warm. The mother said, "He is not here." By the grave was a rose tree that was now in bloom.

And the years passed. The mother often sat out by the grave of an evening, staring away over the mountains that shut everything in. The father stood there for a while if he was passing. But the children kept away, for it was not like elsewhere on earth.

The two sons were growing up now. Soon they were full-grown and tall, and had a new and more spirited air about them than before; but the man and the woman faded away. They became grey and bent; something venerable and tranquil came over them. The father still tried to go hunting with his sons; when the quarry was dangerous it was no longer he but they who fought with it. But the aged mother sat outside the house, she groped with her hand when they came toward her in the evening, her eyes were so tired that she could only see at noonday when the sun was at its height; otherwise it was too dark. She would ask them, "Why is it so dark here?" One autumn she withdrew into the house, lay listening to the wind as to memories from long, long ago. The man sat and held her hand in his, they talked between themselves, it was as though they were again alone here. She wasted away, but her face seemed to become transfigured by light. And one evening she said to them all in her quavering voice, "Now I want to leave this world where I have lived, now I shall go home." And she went away. They buried her in the earth; she was to lie there.

Winter and cold came again, the old man stayed by the hearth, was too feeble to go out. The sons came home with animals, which they would cut up together. With shaking hand he turned the spit, watching how the fire grew redder as the meat was roasted in it. But when the spring came he went into the meadows, gazing at the trees and the grass that were growing green all around him. He stopped by the trees he recognized, he stopped everywhere, recognizing everything. He stopped by the flowers he had picked for her whom he loved the first morning they came here. He stopped by his hunting implements, which were blood-stained because one of the sons had used them. Then he went into the house and lay down, and he said to the sons standing by his deathbed, "Now I must leave this world where I have lived my life, now I must go away. Our home is not here." And he clasped them by the hand until he was dead. They buried him in the earth, as he had bidden them; he wanted to lie there.

Now the old ones were dead. The young ones felt such a strange relief, liberation, as if something had been severed. It was as if life had been freed from something that did not belong to it. They rose early on the morning of the following day. What a scent from the trees that had just come into leaf and from the rain that had fallen in the night! Together they went out, side by side, both tall and newly young; it was joy for the earth to bear them. Now human life was beginning, they went out to take possession of this world.

This book of prose, the first pages of which are reprinted here, was written in 1922 but, in accordance with the author's wishes, has remained unpublished. This extract was made public for the first time on December 10, 1951, when it was read aloud by the author at the banquet given in the Stockholm City Hall in connection with the Nobel Festival.

On the Scales of Osiris

AND the Great King over two kingdoms awakened as from a deep sleep in his grave chamber, which was filled with all the things of the earth, in order to step before the throne of Osiris. Around him there were gathered all the riches of life, all that which is given to the chosen, wagons of cedar inlaid with gold and ivory, war chariots of copper ornamented with reliefs of victory, couches for resting borne by gilded cows with the sun disk between their horns, precious gems in bowls of onyx and jade, shimmering sealed alabaster jars with oils and ointments. Slaves of both sexes carved in wood and small as dolls performed their duties, served marvellous courses, raised the walls of his palace, carried home his quarry and his falcons after the hunt, hoisted his sails on the sacred river. He looked about and did not understand.

At his feet knelt his body servant with his hands pressed against his breast, ready to hear his commands. Ethiopian slaves butchered a sheep and prepared it at the hearth, harvested the fields and drove the oxen at the water wheel. Dancing girls in transparent garments danced for him with their arms lifted above their heads to the music of flutes and harps.

What was this? He could not remember. In a common bowl of clay, unlike anything else there, lay some blackened grains of corn. Servants were occupied in baking bread, wool carding, spinning and weaving. On a basin of gold lay pearls and sparkling precious stones. He understood nothing, did not recognize anything. In the centre his own statue was throned. He did not know who it was. On the pale chalkstone walls of the grave chamber his whole life was pictured, all his power and glory, his victories over his enemies, his armies and chiefs, and he himself triumphant on his chariot riding over the trampled corpses of his foes while the falcon of Horus lifted the looped cross, the sacred mark of life, before his eyes.

What did this mean? He could not explain. The life of the earth lived in all its splendour around him, all that which he had wanted to carry along, all that which he had thought important to have here. All was as he had decided. But he did not now know what the meaning of it was. He stood there and looked about as in an unknown world. His glance was as if touched by a hand which had taken away the interpretation of the pictures; his soul was as a sub-terranean well without surface.

Then his lifeless glance happened to fall on a small gilded image of a woman who radiated light before him through the dimness. She did not awaken any memories in him, not even one. She was as unknown to him as anything there. But within him something moved when he looked at her, as if something were still alive. He went nearer and gazed at the image. She sat with her hands resting on her small knees and her large earthy eyes met his questioning glance. No, he did not know her. But there rose within him something like a mighty wave which filled his breast. He did not know what it was, but it was something great and strange; it gripped him with a secret power. It was something wonderful and incomprehensible, something which lived.

The gold flakes came off when he touched her. Filled his hands with sparkling dust.

Long he stood there in the twilight by her image. Then he lifted his empty eyes and, with his hand on his breast, he entered before the throne of Osiris.

The Strange Country

THE tourist steamer glided along in the pale summer night. The sea was like glass and there was a dying, crimson splendour away in the west where one or two streaks of cloud still glowed long after sunset. All the passengers were out on deck enjoying the sea and sky and the refreshing cool after the day. It was a conducted tour to a distant country famous for its beautiful scenery but most of all for its peculiar manners and customs, which were no longer to be found elsewhere in the world. There had been progress everywhere and an entirely new age had made its appearance. But here everything was just as in days long past. Here, time had apparently stood still. It was the goal for many tourist boats at this time of year, for people who liked the remote and romantically picturesque, and for others who just thought they should see this curious little country about which they had heard and who took the chance of going there for their holiday, especially as the sea trip in itself meant a pleasant rest and recreation now in the summer. But many scientists, too, went there to study the customs and social order of a bygone age, outmoded conceptions and ideas once held by humanity and long since abandoned, but surviving here with stubborn conservatism and on account of the country's isolated position. What could otherwise only be read about in learned works was here disclosed and accessible as fully live study material.

In the general consciousness there was, without a doubt, something faintly ridiculous about the little country and its inhabitants; people were apt to give a wry smile when it cropped up in conversation and the expression "That's like in Liberania!" was often used when things were all at sixes and sevens, though people as a rule had rather a hazy notion of the real meaning of the phrase and only knew that there was supposed to be a country called that. But it was a harmless joke. No one really had anything against this Liberania, which existed somewhere far off the beaten track and outside the mighty stream of current events, living its naïve, old-fashioned life remote from the big world. Otherwise it could easily have been conquered, it would have been a simple matter for one of its powerful neighbours, who were all armed to the teeth and whose famous child-armies alone would have sufficed to carry out an annexation. But it was left in peace and allowed to keep its manners and customs and its quaint little independence. Had its position been in the least important strategically, it would naturally have been annexed. But this was not the case. In the modern shaping of the world, far-off Liberania was of no importance whatsoever. Its only interest was purely cultural and historical, having preserved its character from a forgotten, long-departed age when everything had been different from now and from which there were no other memories extant. It was kept as a curiosity, as a kind of natural reserve.

The passengers were genuinely pleased to be going there. They made the journey for various reasons, but they could not be called a mixed company, on the contrary they comprised a very correct group of people, all extraordinarily like each other. They talked about the trip and the weather and delighted in the strange fact that it never grew dark. It was a new and wonderful experience for them. At eleven o'clock, however, they were all ordered below deck in order to get some sleep. And it was nice to go to bed. It was advisable to be well rested for what lay in store tomorrow morning, when they were to arrive.

The boat tied up in the harbour in the forenoon. It was
a strange and animated scene which unfolded there on the
quay. People were walking or running past each other just
as they pleased, there was no sign of any soldiers or other
uniformed men. They moved about unconcernedly and
defencelessly in the small space where the ship was
moored. A boy who was loafing about caught the hawser
—though it seemed nothing to do with him—and threw
it round the bollard, on which he then sat down to finish
his cigarette. It escaped the notice of most, but those with
a practised eye instantly saw in it a characteristic of the
country. The crowd on the quay pushed and jostled, did
whatever they liked, as though they were at complete
liberty, it seemed. At least it was impossible to detect any
particular rules to which the whole thing conformed.
Actually, they all looked bright and alert, there was
nothing strikingly antiquated about them at a cursory
glance from this distance. But degeneration was apparent
in the poor bearing throughout, especially noticeable in
the men; it gave a deplorable impression, all the more
deplorable as they were really quite tall of stature. They
were curiously dressed, in a kind of short coat which
was only buttoned at the bottom or else left quite open;
the trousers, instead of being tucked into boots, hung loose
round the legs; on the back of the head they wore a
peculiar, old-fashioned, high-crowned headgear which,
from what one heard later, was called a hat and which
they swung once in the air when they passed each other,
something which looked quite comical. A picturesque,
colourful touch was their shirts, which were now white,
now blue, now pink, or else striped, blue and white
stripes, yellow and green stripes, and which were particularly effective as the men, because of the heat, went about
in their shirt-sleeves. This also revealed that some of them
kept their trousers up with braces, just like infants. This
could not have been a mere coincidence, as there was

something undoubtedly childish about them altogether, in the good-natured expression on their faces and their entire behaviour.

That was about all one could observe here from the boat. The gangway was lowered and everyone marched ashore, to be greeted with gay and polite smiles by the hospitable people, who derived a good income from the stream of tourists from the big world outside.

When the strangers had been installed in their barracks, which the steamship company had had built in order that they might feel more at home in the far-off land, they set off into the town in smaller detachments under officers detailed for the purpose. It was the country's capital, where the small government had its seat, but the streets basked peacefully in the sun with only an odd police constable here and there on a street-corner or a few who were on traffic duty in the open places. No proper police force could be seen, nobody looked after you, each one apparently had to manage as best he could by himself. There were now a lot of inhabitants to be seen like those down at the harbour; they all seemed to be busy with their small private affairs, dressed in their antiquated costumes, which made a quaint, captivating scene of national life. In the main streets people drifted along in disorderly groups and more often than not bumped into each other because they were not looking straight ahead in line of march but turned round or simply stood still for a while, as the fancy took them—collisions which gave rise to that comical swing with their headgear, which was obviously some mark of civility. On the other hand, there was no form of salutation, at least none that was uniform and laid down by law. There was no raising of the arm or fist, they waved with their hands just anyhow and called out something unintelligible to each other. It was later explained that "Hallo," "Cheerio" and "So long" were uttered on such occasions. On further inquiry, however, these expressions turned out to be devoid of any essential meaning or deeper significance in their lives. In a similar way, there was a marked lack of ordered conditions in general. Everything happened rather haphazardly, with no sign of any guiding principle behind it all. Life ran its course and people seemed just to make the best of it. Things were arranged and done more or less as they fell out, with an attractive kind of carelessness. The whole thing was extremely interesting and strange. So romantic! was the exclamation often heard in the troop as it marched through the city, now and then having to halt at something particularly remarkable.

These first superficial impressions were not misleading. During the days that followed, one got to know the country and people better, came in contact with the inhabitants and their peculiar, antiquated world. One often got surprisingly lucid answers to one's questions, in so far as the population, palpably rather ignorant, could make themselves understood in one's langauge. Their own language was impossible to understand or express oneself in, though apparently they themselves spoke it fluently. It often proved difficult, however, to gain any really sure idea of the prevailing state of affairs, for if you asked one person about something, he would explain it in his way, and if you asked another he had a completely different opinion. In fact, it even happened that the same person expressed two viewpoints about exactly the same thing, one at the beginning and one at the end of his discourse. It was most odd and confusing. But if you pointed it out to him, at first he would look blank and then just give that good-natured, disarming smile of theirs.

Troublesome though this was, and thereby difficult to to get a plain answer and really find out about them, this peculiarity of theirs was far from being without interest. In *its* way it was very revealing—in the end perhaps more revealing than anything else. They lacked in fact a guiding train of thought, into which casual and individual thinking could be led and cease to be private property. They had no common and ever-present ideal which gave a fixed norm to their sayings and actions. And they had not the energy, as it were, to intervene sufficiently; they often left life untouched in a curiously helpless fashion. There was something almost frightening about this, one was seized by a distressing feeling of emptiness. All in all, there was no deep meaning in their lives—they were just born, they lived and died.

When you tried to explain this to them, they said that they didn't understand what you meant. And they probably didn't, either. They were too primitive to understand anything other than what was purely self-evident.

But apart from this they were very nice people. One liked it surprisingly well there, even though one couldn't approve of anything. It was really a very successful holiday trip, the ideal place in which to relax a trifle.

One felt so well and rested. The very atmosphere had a beneficial effect and made one almost hilarious. Even the officers unbent and sometimes let slip joking and quite unnecessary remarks. Discipline was also relaxed slightly and more and more often one was allowed to walk at ease in the troop. In fact, individuals were even allowed at last to leave the barracks on parole, although many did not avail themselves of this as they didn't enjoy it. But others, and by degrees the majority, thought it was very interesting and took increasing pleasure in it. They began strolling about the town on their own like quite ordinary people.

The first few times it was a very strange feeling. One floated, one seemed to become air and move to and fro like a disembodied spirit, as though blown by a faint, imperceptible wind. And one walked along thinking of this and that and sometimes of nothing at all. It felt most peculiar. But not entirely pleasant until one got used to it.

All kinds of things were permissible. One didn't know how to behave in different situations. The natives took this state of affairs as a matter of course, they moved about, quite at home, with an astonishing, deft agility. They couldn't understand one's unfamiliarity and sometimes smiled at one's awkwardness.

Everything was utter confusion. There seemed to be no definite rules about anything, or if there were that didn't mean that they were followed. For instance, it was surely forbidden to cross the street except at certain prescribed places, but one often saw a native who, when there was no car or other vehicle coming in either direction, simply made for the other side. It looked so funny. Among the strangers there were several who were almost tempted to do the same, so that they could boast about it when they got home. But when it came to it they just couldn't, however much they wanted to. There was something after all that went against the grain.

But after a little practice one gradually learnt to manage quite well. One watched what the others did in this strange world and copied as much of it as was suitable. And once having got the hang of everything, one really enjoyed it and found it very exciting.

Picture postcards were sent home: You'd never dream how odd it is here! You should have come too! Awfully interesting. We go about free just like savages and have great fun. How are things with you?

In the restaurants everyone sat close together and one could talk to those who had some knowledge of one's language. Once having got into conversation one could hear the most incredible things about conditions in their country. And the very sight of the public at such a place was fascinating. It was a motley of flaxen-haired, black-haired and redheads, a colourful, changing spectacle of a curious wildness. A flaxen-head could be seen talking to someone with black hair, as though it were nothing, and a swarthy man would sit flirting with a lovely blond woman, who apparently had no objection to letting him treat her just as he liked. It was strange and fantastic. Occasionally it would happen that some of the tourists felt nauseated and had to go out for a while, but they came back before long and sat down again so as not to miss the unique experience.

Otherwise one passed the time in poking about sight-seeing, as tourists do. And there were plenty of curious and instructive things to see. One very popular amusement, for instance, was a visit to the old-fashioned institution in an ancient building where the inhabitants ruled their little country, decided how they wanted to run it—entirely on their own. There they said whatever they liked about their government or anything else, made no bones about anything. It was so funny to see their self-assurance as they thumped their fists on the table and spoke their minds in a loud voice. And they got their own way, no question of that! It was an awfully amusing business. When, for instance, one of them stood with his hands in his pockets and abused the whole bag of tricks so that the rafters rang —it was a laughable sight.

But the funniest thing of all was that they thought all their oddities quite natural. They *themselves* had no idea that they were strange.

While the rank and file of the tourists sauntered about in this way making their quite ordinary and superficial observations, the scientists among them were busy eagerly making the most remarkable discoveries in their respective fields. There was no question here of any surface, but of penetrating right down to the foundation of everything and exposing it. And in this they succeeded entirely. The ethnographists took detailed measurements of the shape of the head and angle of the face, the distance between the cheekbones, determined whether the people were dolicho-cephalic or brachycephalic, and so on—the good-natured inhabitants submitted willingly, just smiled broadly as the scientists got busy with their ingenious apparatuses. Unfortunately, however, they arrived at no definite result. There turned out to be every possible kind of facial angle, from the very blunt to the very sharp, and long skulls and short skulls and those that were neither short nor long—all jumbled together. It was the same as with everything else in the country, there was no order. This, however, was the very thing which put the scientists on the right track, as so often when a difficulty or incongruity leads to big scientific discoveries. They found that the underlying cause of this irregularity was the fact that they formed no definite race, at least not in a real, modern sense but only quite generally or purely biologically, that is to say they formed what one might call a natural race. And this was what was so extremely interesting. Here, apparently, was the only place on earth where such a natural race still existed, while all other races had long ago been refined and become purebred, had been submitted to rational culture. Here, therefore, was the basic reason for their dissimilarity from other races, which even the untrained eye had noticed up to a point. In all, they had no appearance in common, each one looked just as he liked or as it chanced, which was a typical sign of degeneration.

On the whole they were, of course, very degenerated—otherwise they would not have stood still at this stage of development but would have progressed with the rest of the world. Outwardly they looked healthy, to be sure, but it is easy to be misled by something which has nothing to do with the problem as such. Besides, their all too marked vivacity was undoubtedly of a nervous nature and served to mask the inferiority complex from which they naturally suffered.

Degeneration was also explained by the very fact that they had lived in peace for several hundred years and so the weaker individuals had never been weeded out by the efficacy of modern warfare in this respect. As a result, there were weaklings everywhere who impaired the race, whereas they could all have been very strong. And people were allowed to marry almost anyone they liked, so that one often saw ill-matched couples who should instantly have been separated. They also lacked the simplest form of rational race hygiene.

The women were undeniably handsome and erotically stimulating, but this was unfortunately due to the fact that they did not bear enough children. There were really no more children born than was necessary. One did see a lot of youngsters, but statistics showed that there were not enough. Owing to a lack of surplus population the nation no longer had any healthy power of expansion and sank deeper and deeper into decay.

They were an impotent, inept and on the whole very depraved people.

The psychologists' intelligence tests, made with the greatest possible accuracy on a large number of cases picked at random from all strata of the population, also gave the only result to be expected. Their branch of science met with no set-backs and the outcome was soon quite definite, though disappointing. The investigation clearly showed a marked subnormality all round, they were almost semi-idiots the lot of them. These observations, when reported to them, aroused great mirth and gave rise to many infantile jokes which further confirmed the accuracy of the tests.

The population altogether showed a trait of undoubted puerility, and the seeds of this were obviously sown in early childhood by a misguided upbringing. The children were retarded by being allowed to run about and play with each other as they liked, without earnestness and discipline. They were not taken charge of in any proper units. They were given no exercises whatever of a military kind. It was noted with interest, however, that on their own account

they made themselves small wooden rifles, bows and cata-
pults which they practised with—a tendency which was
subsequently thwarted, however.

If the inhabitants were thus on a particularly low level,
both physically and mentally, they could not be denied a
certain culture, as the scientists in this field confirmed
during their investigations. The fact that they had remained at a stage of development long since abandoned
elsewhere was another matter, and anyway this was just
what was so valuable to research. A thoughtless person
might be inclined to regard the country's simple inhabitants with a condescending smile, but science saw
these things with another eye and admitted that even they
were bearers of a kind of culture. They had their
humanistic and well-meaning institutions, their old-
fashioned ethics which after all must indicate a certain
modest stage of culture at which the rest of the world had
once been. They had their laws, which, however lax and
obscure, were undeniably based on a certain conception
of justice. They had their schools, where the growing
generation was educated, even if wrongly. According to
reports, they there acquired knowledge which had been
rejected by the rest of the world as misleading several
centuries ago.

There was also a so-called higher mental culture.
Antiquated fields of science, with the most curious methods
which had been discarded long ago, clung to a languishing
life, being without encouragement and support from the
real centres of culture. One would encounter their singular
representatives, mostly old men with a gentle and meek
smile, bent and grey and awfully friendly and obliging, but
quite impossible to reason with, as they were utterly
obsessed by their fixed ideas regarding their precious
"science"—one had a feeling of being in the presence of
medieval astrologists and alchemists brooding over their
dark secrets. It was distressing to note from their many

hesitant, oddly diffuse statements that at the same time they lived in constant doubt as to the accuracy of their observations. But it would have been unjust not to admit that there was a certain degree of culture even in a science like that.

There was also a kind of primitive literature, though quite chaotic and confused. As was only to be expected, their writers were allowed to write anything at all that they happened to think of, just as the fancy took them. They chose their subjects themselves, in other words, did not receive them from a uniform and organizing centre, nor did they compose their books jointly in groups of five or ten, but each one made them up out of his own head. And the results were in keeping. Their works never reached the outside world, as they were utterly without interest in their barbaric originality. There was also the press, although it played no part in the national life as the various newspapers more often than not expressed different views, so that it was useless as a moulder of opinion.

But even such literature and such a press must be said to indicate a certain culture, though at an early stage. Generally speaking, it could not be denied that they were a cultured race in *their* way, even if not in the modern and stricter sense. Their viewpoint was not altogether contemptible, especially bearing in mind their almost complete isolation from the rest of the world. One had to take a broader view of things and realize that humanity had not always been on the same level as now. These were the conclusions reached in this respect.

But the really remarkable discoveries were made by one or two eminent historians with an excellent all-round education and piercing insight who had made the trip in order to confirm their theories, which they also did. Behind the little country's confused notions and apparently inexplicable, disordered state of affairs they found a peculiar train of thought which led as a guiding thread through the

whole curious maze and which, for lack of a stricter
scientific term, they chose to call for the time being "the
idea of freedom." The inhabitants went about quite at
liberty. And not from any slack indifference, as one might
be inclined to think, but from a real inner need—and, as
was soon discovered, because of a firmly rooted tradition.
They wanted to try to think freely and brooked no regula-
tions whatever which were designed to stop them. They
had free research in all fields, a quest for truth which
no law could restrict. They upheld independence, inviol-
ability and the right of the individual with an almost
fanatic stubbornness. In mysteriously coloured and incomprehensible metaphysics of great obscurity they even
seemed to want to uphold the liberty of life itself and
maintained that it should not be hampered unnecessarily
but left alone as far as possible. In fact, from all appear-
ances they taught that human life had its own values, apart
from its value in the society to which it belonged, and that
this value was of a higher and more primary nature.

This idea of liberty made itself strongly felt everywhere,
in their feelings and actions, in their private and public
life. It was neither a chance, unhistorical curiosity nor,
originally, the property of this nation; it had very old,
ramified traditions which were lost far back in the mists of
time. Men really had thought like this at one time, they
had fumbled and fought their way along on these lines,
seeking, in their fashion, truth and justice and a certain
meaning in existence, according to the notions of the age.
They had tried to apply such a metaphysical value to life;
a similar train of thought, which was still apparent here in
all its oddity and strange, characteristic consequences, had
actually existed and been quite widespread; such a science,
of which these grey-haired old eccentrics were the last
moribund representatives, had once been cultivated in the
world at large. The whole of this singular culture had long
since vanished in the countries where it had originally had

its home, but in this remote little country it had survived and could still be plainly discerned in all its essentials; just as on one or two previous occasions it had been possible to find, in similar isolated places, the living remnants—in misunderstood and distorted forms perhaps of cultures that were otherwise completely dead and forgotten.

Sensing, rightly, that this should also be the case here, and seeing the issue at large, these historians had come here with a purpose and had been richly rewarded for their pains. It was indeed a triumph of research, and a triumph for the school of thought they represented and which was in open opposition to an older, more stereotyped conception of history.

"The idea of liberty," however, was not quite the right term and had to be replaced by something else, implying as it did a *contradictio in adjecto*, for freedom must involve a lack of any guiding idea. When one is not guided by any really fixed idea, one is free. Freedom as such, therefore, implies this very lack of ideas. But otherwise it was right. And this formal contradiction could easily be omitted when the wealth of study material was sifted and re-touched.

There was really something magnificent about this mighty thread leading back into time. This perspective had a deeply stimulating effect on the scientist and had a strange fascination. It was of the utmost importance to him that such a people actually still existed. They must at all costs be preserved just as unspoilt as hitherto and not influenced by the ideas of the new age, so that they would always be there in their present state for scientists to refer to. To be indignant about this, as some were, was merely a ridiculous sentimentality of the kind which all too often hampered science in its work. That must not happen here. It should even be expressly forbidden for tourists to speak in front of the native inhabitants about conditions in the rest of the world, in order not to inveigle them into forsaking their antiquated mode of thinking.

This, therefore, was what the scientists accomplished during their stay in the country. It goes without saying that they were satisfied and proud of the results.

All were satisfied, in fact, learned and unlearned alike. They had seen a people who were different from others, which nowadays was very difficult and which not many of their acquaintances had done. They had gone for long excursions in glorious, unspoilt scenery which exceeded all expectations as regards originality and wildness and which left an unforgettable memory. There was one thing really magnificent in this country, and that was the scenery. One felt fit as a fiddle and exhilarated in quite a special way. One had gained health and strength and breathed a pure and stimulating air.

The only thing one had missed was a little festivity now and then. There were no parades, and one did miss those after a while; not at first, but as time went on it seemed boring never to see any. But in an exotic setting one is always seized at times by such a feeling of monotony. One had not been able to help experiencing a certain sense of insecurity either, as was only natural in a country where not even a part of the population was armed. But everything had gone well, there had been no mishaps, everyone had been so nice and friendly. All things considered, they were a particularly good-natured and pleasant people and one had got on very well with them.

Now the day had come for the trip home and the tourists embarked in the steamer. The weather was fine, as it had been the whole time, the sea was calm and one stood leaning over the railing, talking of one's impressions and experiences and of what a wonderful time one had had, or just amusing oneself with anything at all; the days passed in the most agreeable way. And then one morning the ship arrived and one was received by the authorities and everything else that was so familiar. Several who had let fall unseemly remarks during customs examination or who had forgotten to make the official salute were waved good-bye to as they left with special transport, and then, happy and content, one got into the coaches reserved by the travel bureau and settled down comfortably in one's corner.

It had been a wonderful trip. But it was nice to be home again after all.